GLORK PATROL

ON THE BAD PLANET

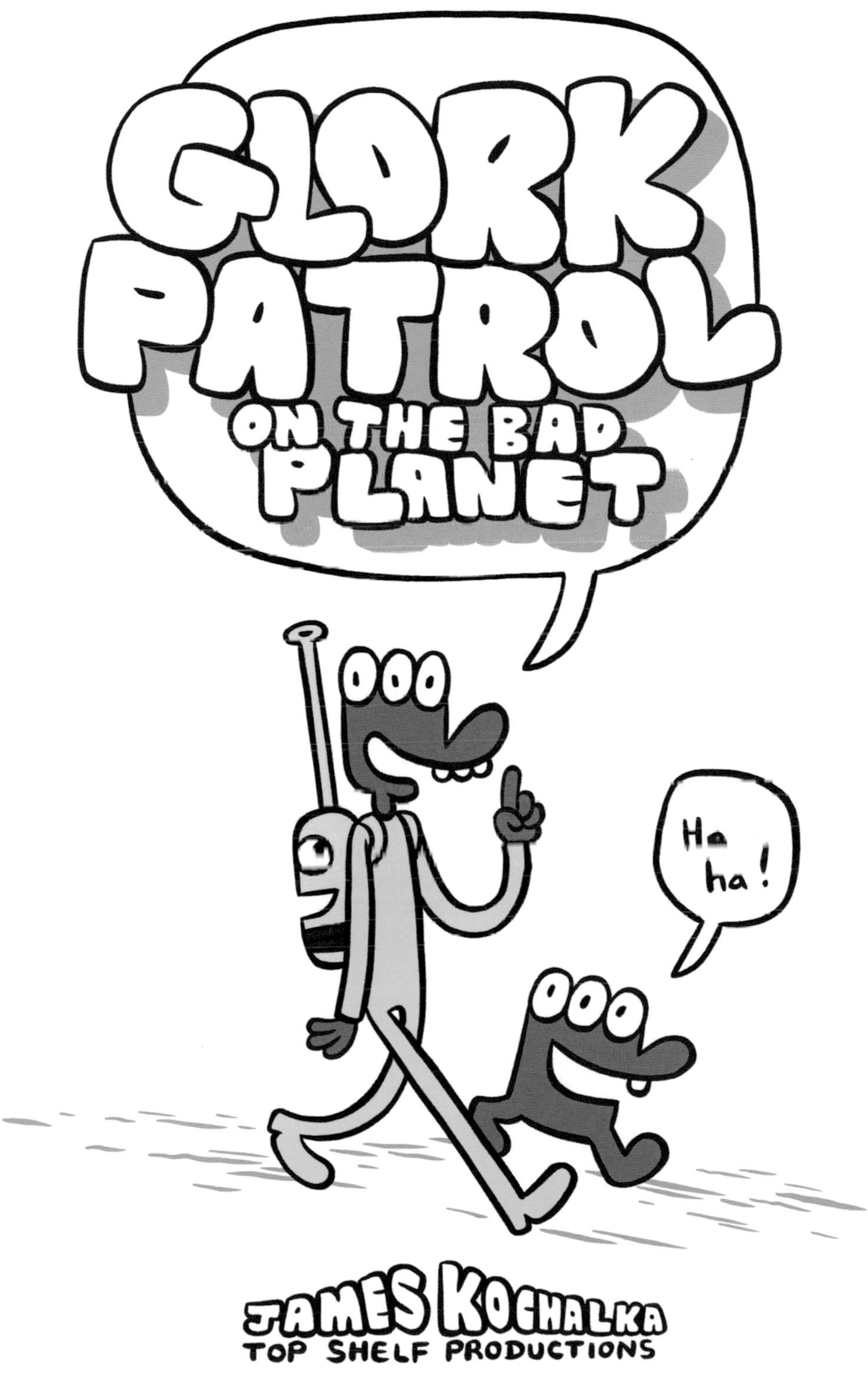
Ha ha!

JAMES KOCHALKA

TOP SHELF PRODUCTIONS

FOR ELI & OLIVER,
THOSE KIDS WHO
CALLED ME DA-DA.

You should also Read
the Glorkian Warrior
trilogy, the Dragon Puncher
books, and the Johnny Boo
Series... all by
James Kochalka!

AND don't forget the video game
GLORKIAN WARRIOR: THE TRIALS OF GLORK
WWW.GLORKIANWARRIOR.COM

Glork Patrol (Book One) © 2020 James Kochalka.

ISBN 978-1-60309-475-7   24 23 22 21 20   1 2 3 4 5

Published by Top Shelf Productions, an imprint of IDW Publishing, a division of Idea and Design Works, LLC. Offices: Top Shelf Productions, c/o Idea & Design Works, LLC, 2765 Truxtun Road, San Diego, CA 92106. Top Shelf Productions®, the Top Shelf logo, Idea and Design Works®, and the IDW logo are registered trademarks of Idea and Design Works, LLC. All Rights Reserved. With the exception of small excerpts of artwork used for review purposes, none of the contents of this publication may be reprinted without the permission of IDW Publishing. IDW Publishing does not read or accept unsolicited submissions of ideas, stories, or artwork.

Printed in China.

Editor-in-chief: Chris Staros.
Edited by Leigh Walton.
Designed by Gilberto Lazcano & Tara McCrillis.

Visit our online catalog
at topshelfcomix.com

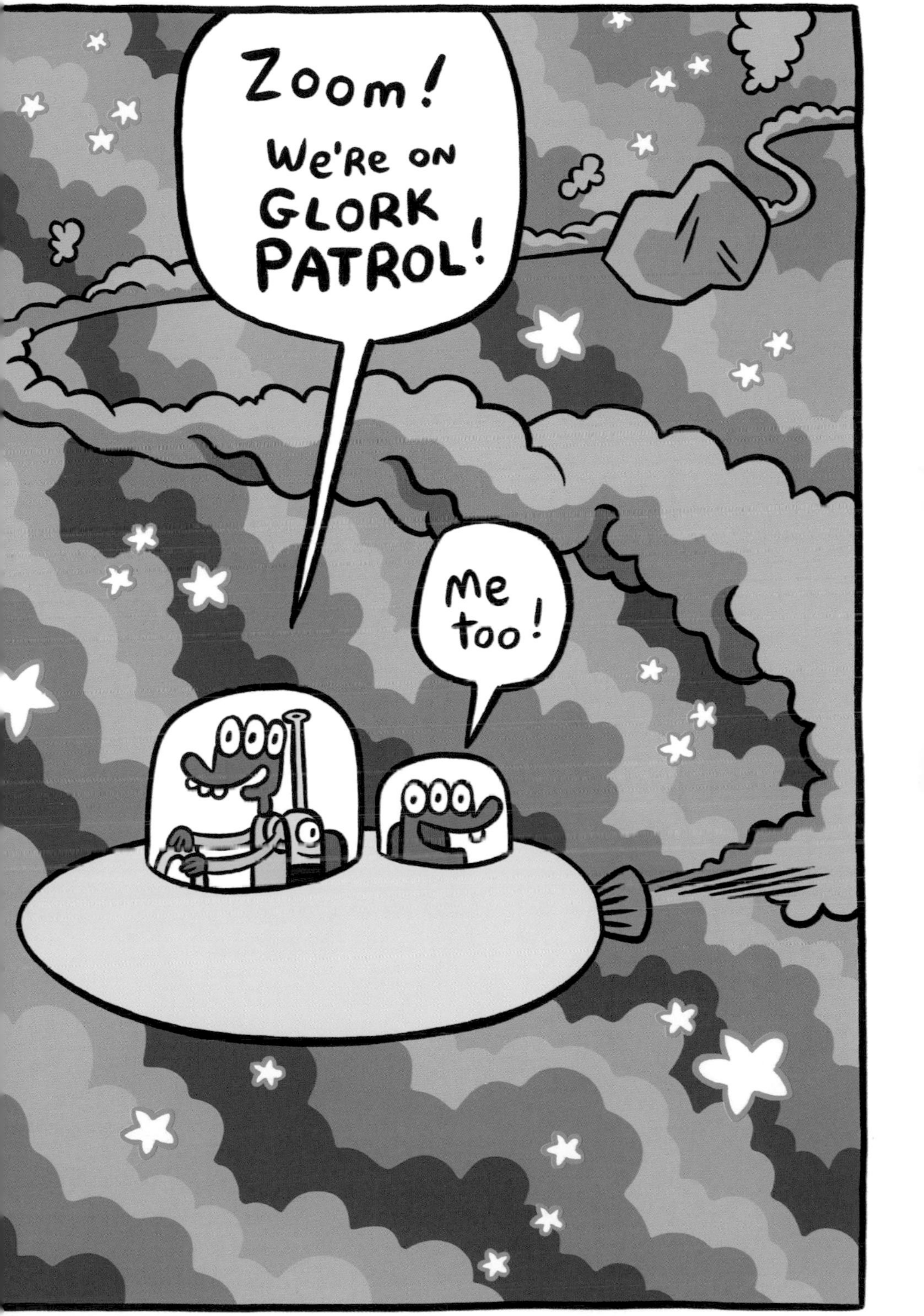
Zoom! We're on GLORK PATROL!
Me too!

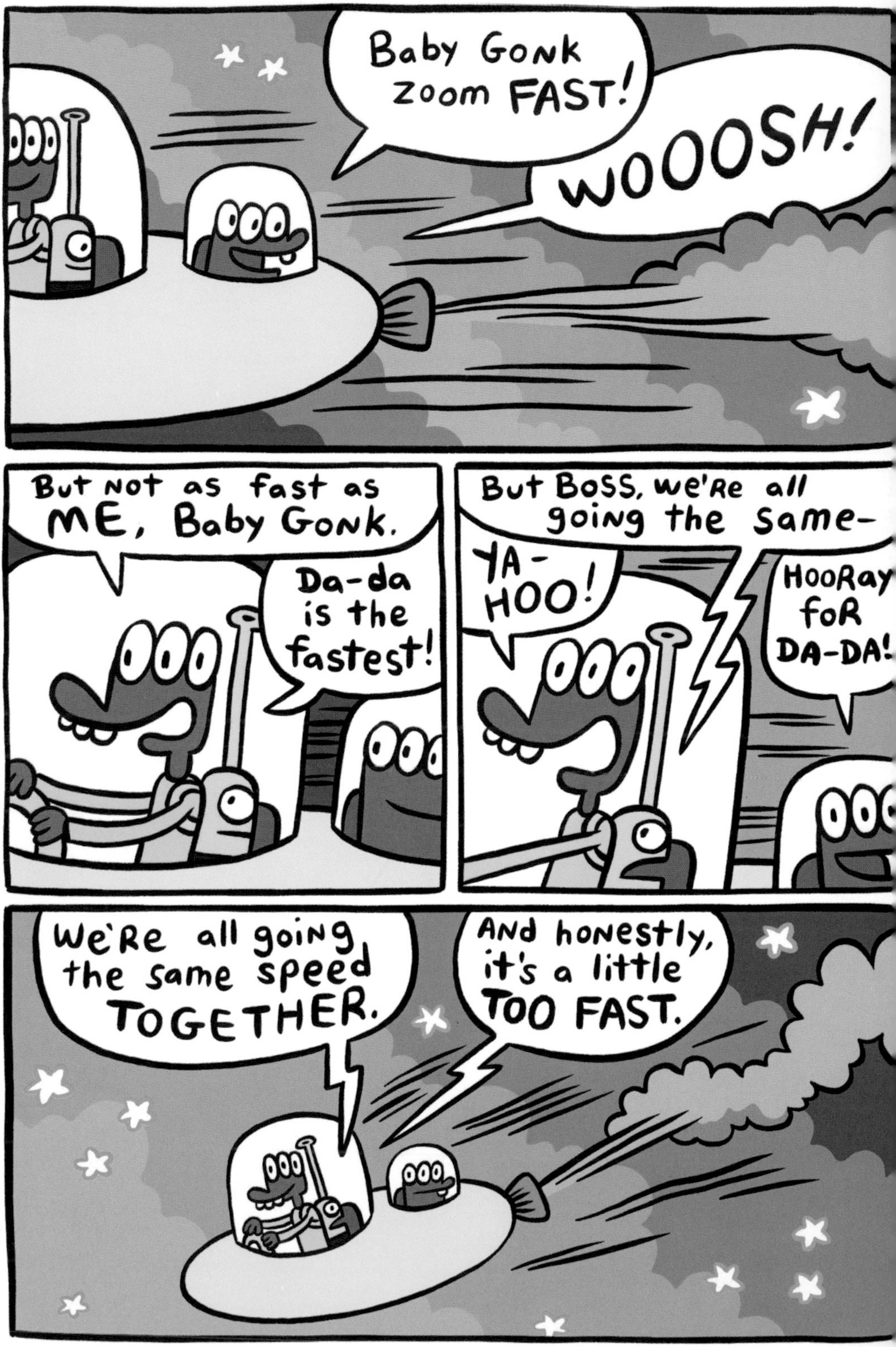

Baby Gonk zoom FAST!
WOOOSH!
But NOT as fast as ME, Baby Gonk.
Da-da is the fastest!
But BOSS, we're all going the same-
YA-HOO!
HOORay foR DA-DA!
We're all going the same speed TOGETHER.
AND honestly, it's a little TOO FAST.

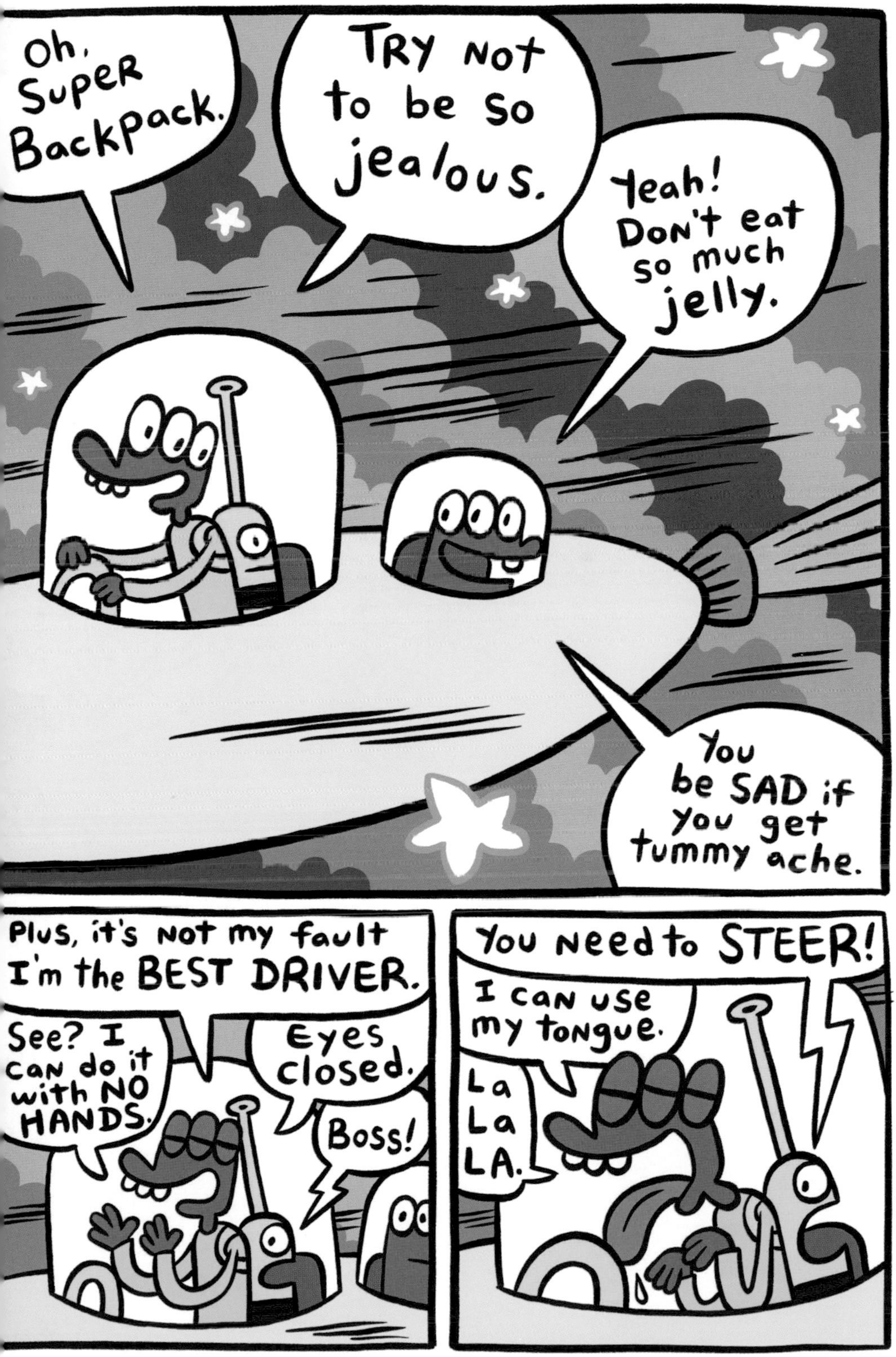
Oh, Super Backpack.
TRY not to be so jealous.
Yeah! Don't eat so much jelly.
You be SAD if you get tummy ache.
Plus, it's not my fault I'm the BEST DRIVER.
See? I can do it with NO HANDS.
Eyes closed.
Boss!
You need to STEER!
I can use my tongue.
La La LA.

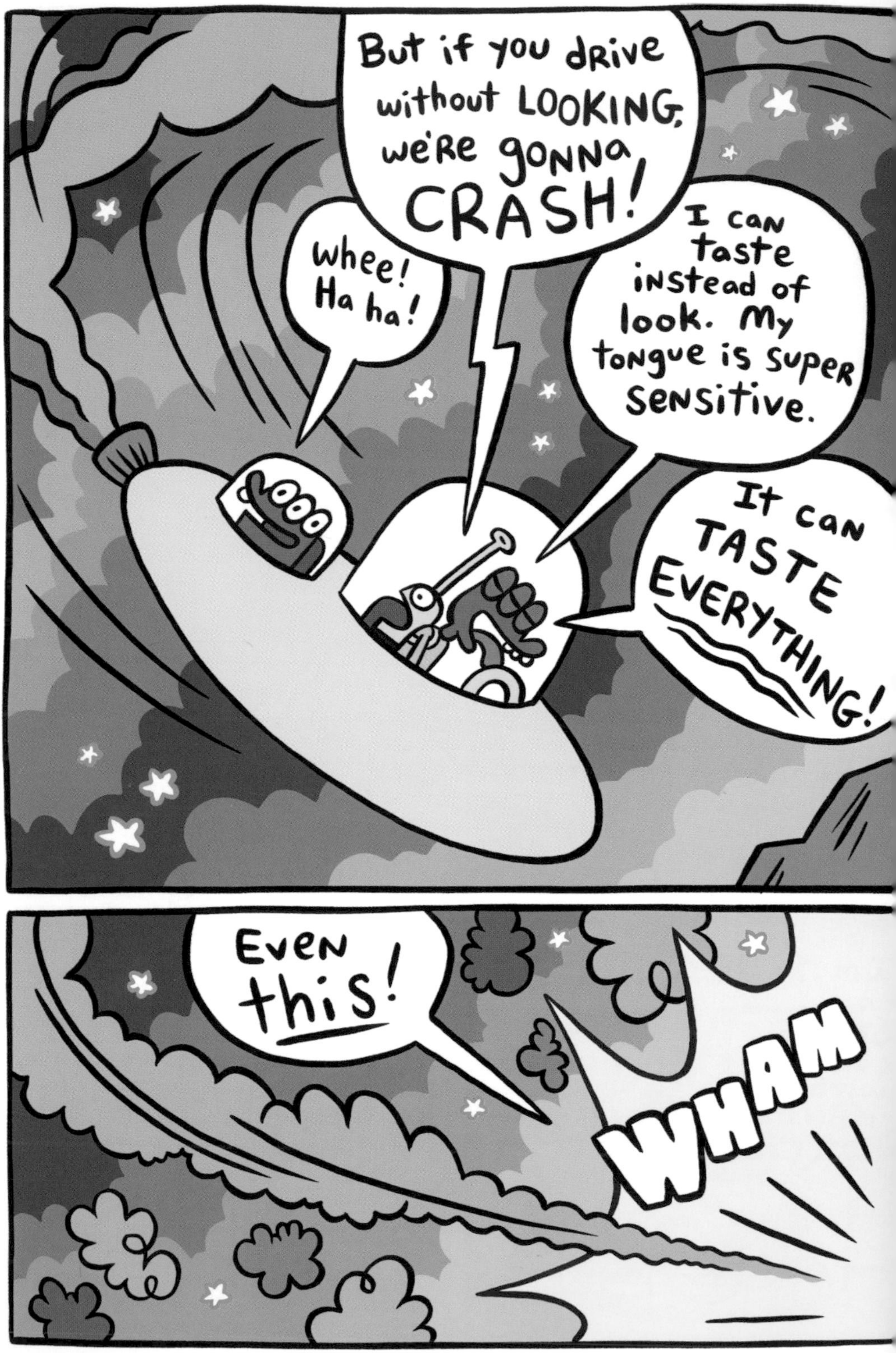

But if you drive without LOOKING, we're gonna CRASH!
Whee! Ha ha!
I can taste instead of look. My tongue is super sensitive.
It can TASTE EVERYTHING!
Even this!
WHAM

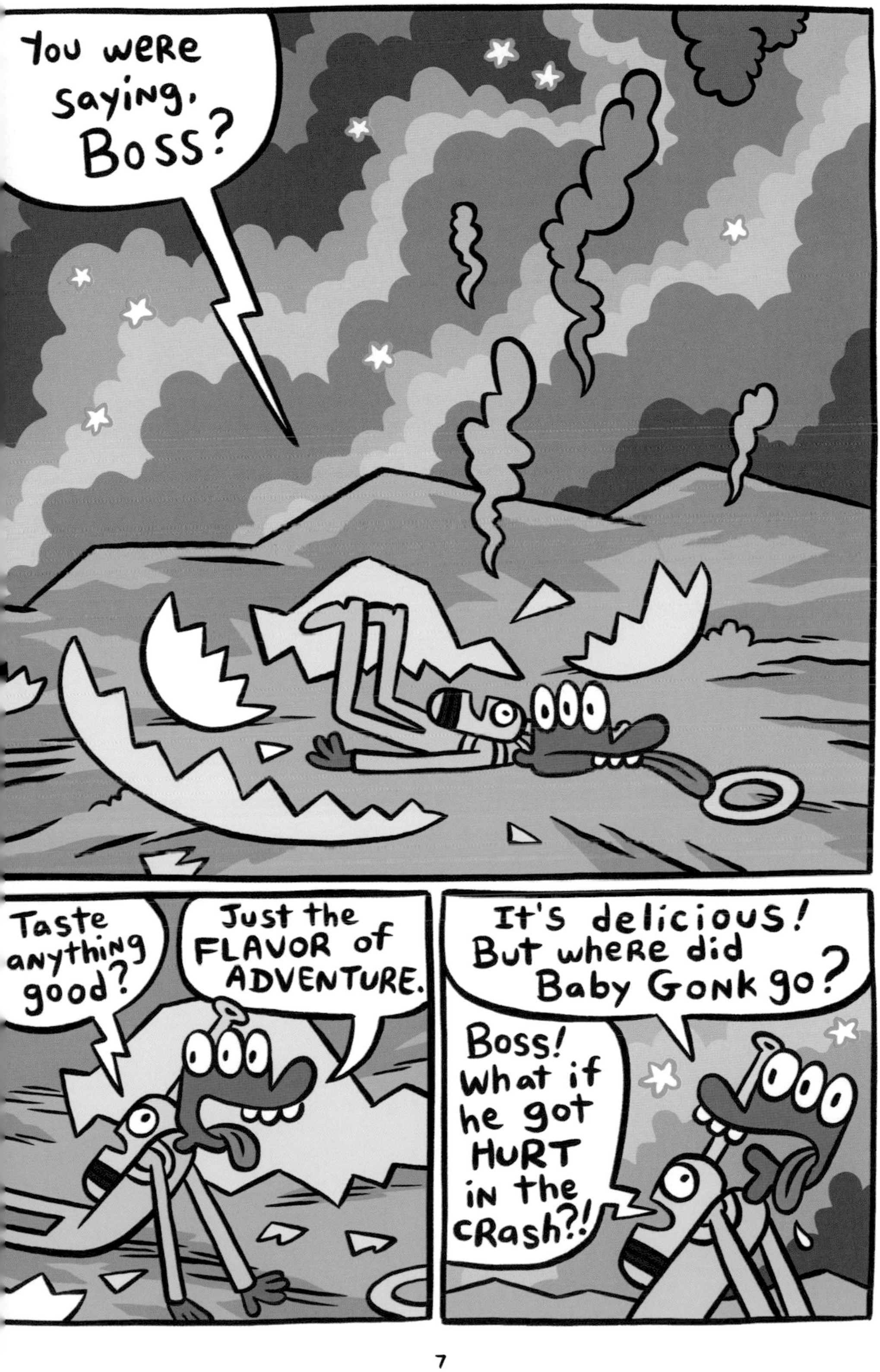
You were saying, Boss?
Taste anything good?
Just the FLAVOR of ADVENTURE.
It's delicious! But where did Baby Gonk go?
Boss! What if he got HURT in the crash?!

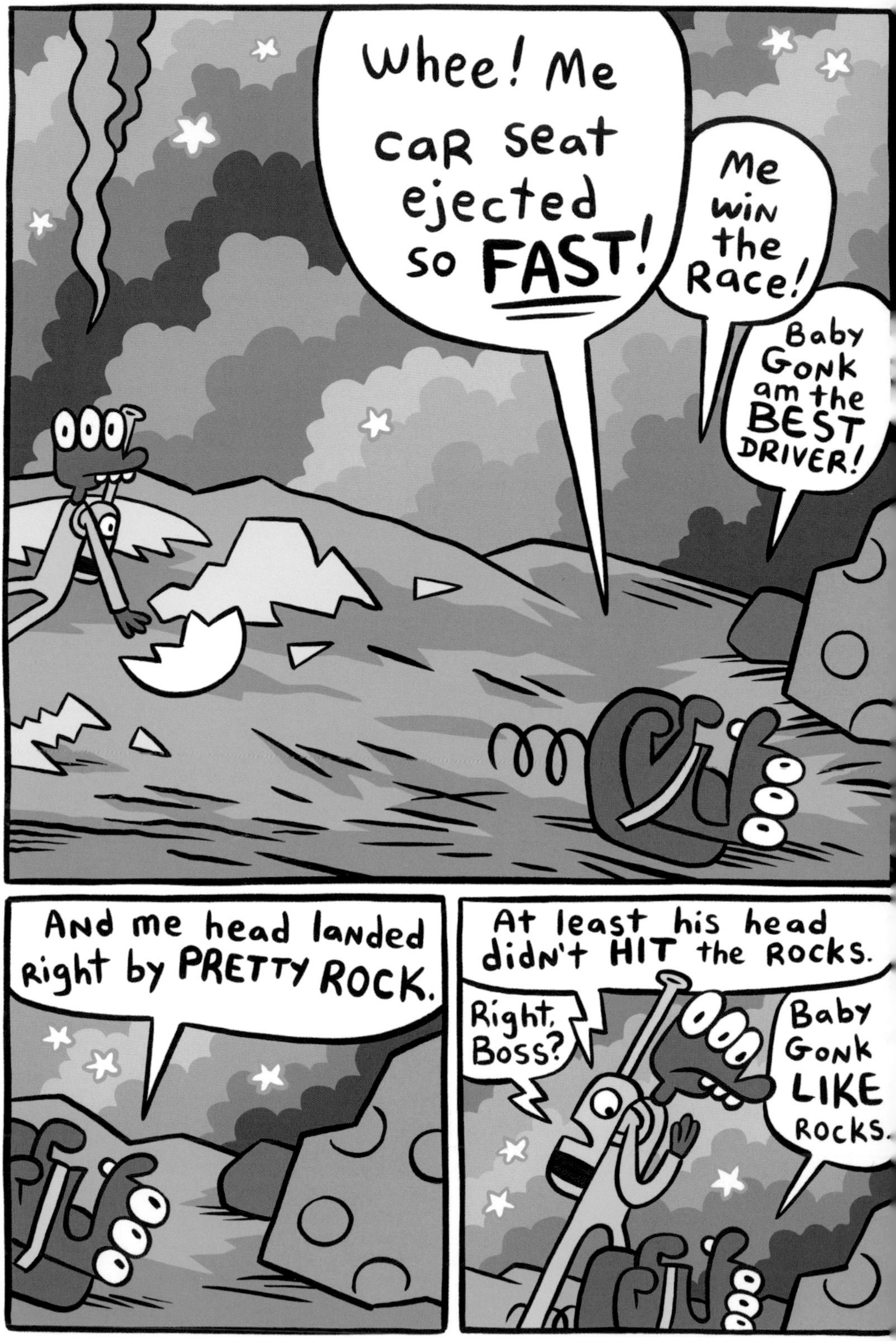
Whee! Me car seat ejected so FAST!
Me win the Race!
Baby Gonk am the BEST DRIVER!
And me head landed right by PRETTY ROCK.
At least his head didn't HIT the ROCKS.
Right, Boss?
Baby Gonk LIKE ROCKS.

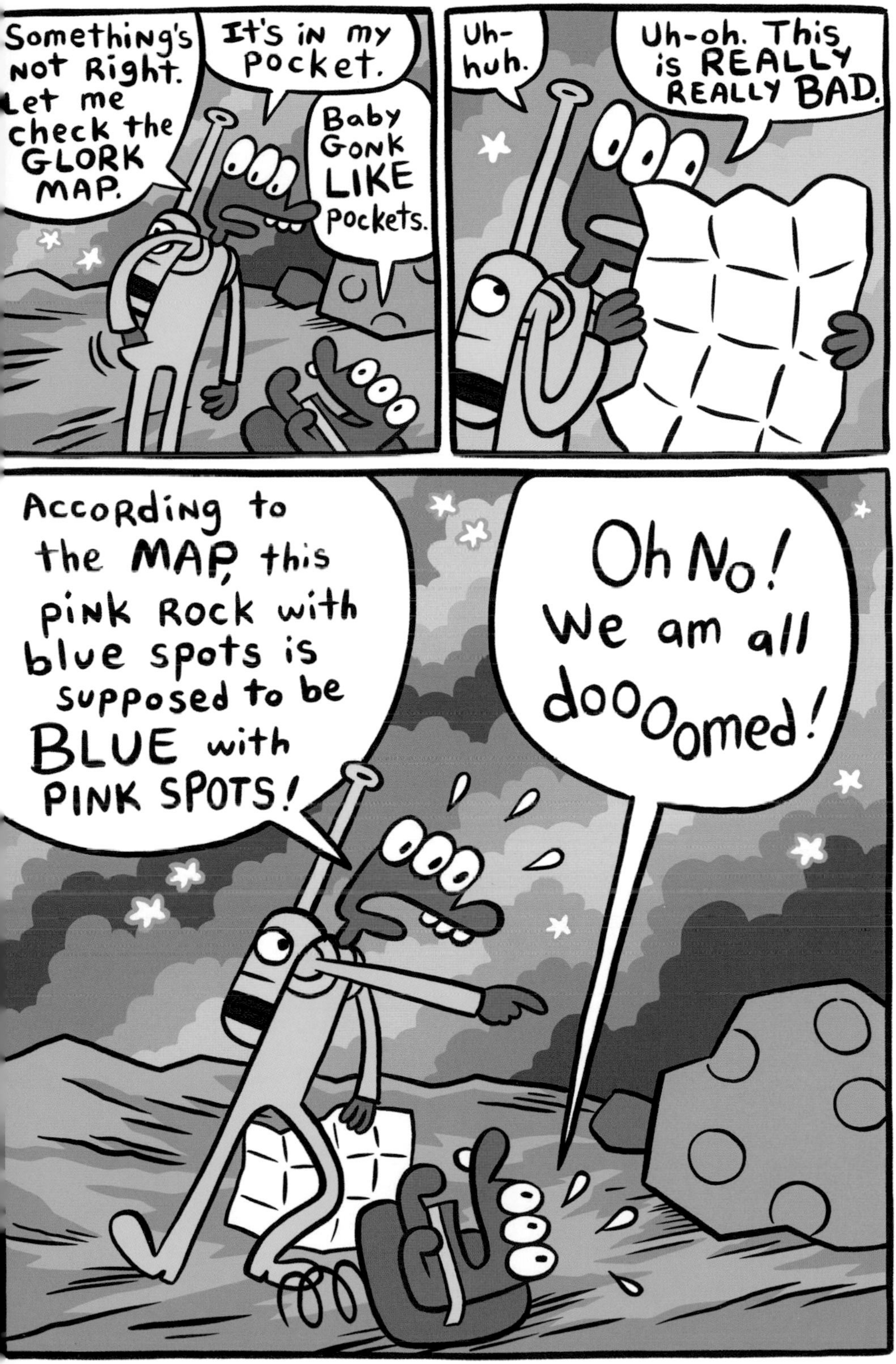
Something's not Right. Let me check the GLORK MAP.
It's in my pocket.
Baby GONK LIKE pockets.
Uh-huh.
Uh-oh. This is REALLY REALLY BAD.
According to the MAP, this pink Rock with blue spots is supposed to be BLUE with PINK SPOTS!
Oh No! We am all doooomed!

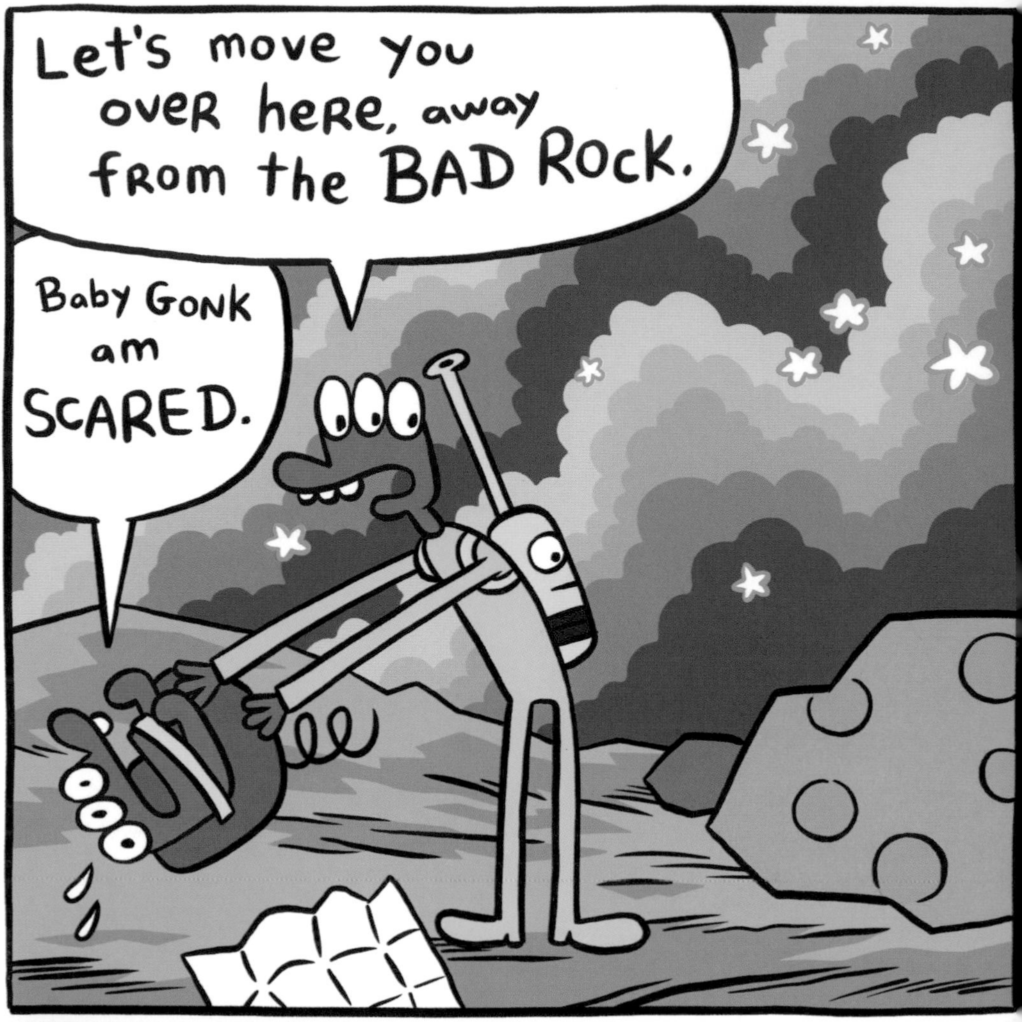
Let's move you over here, away from the BAD ROCK.
Baby GONK am SCARED.

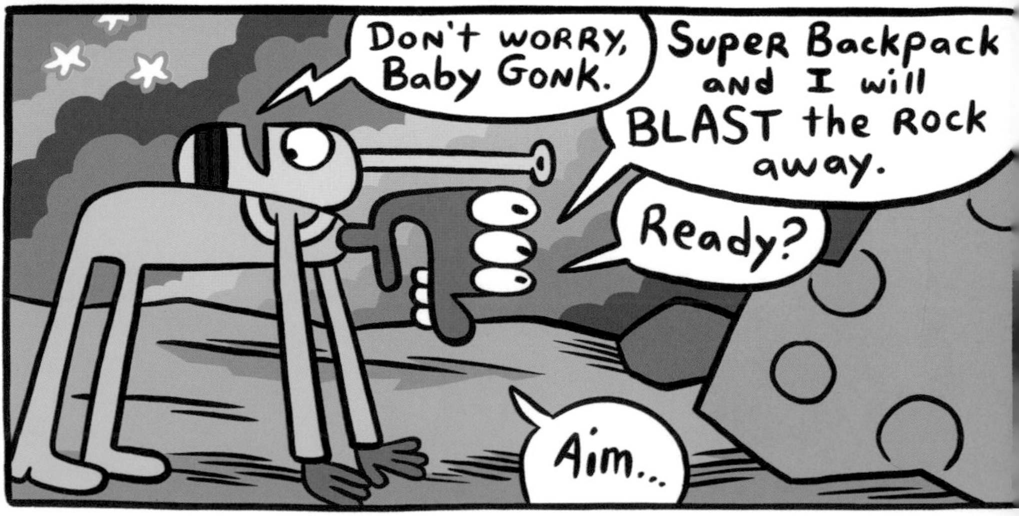
DON'T WORRY, Baby GONK.
Super Backpack and I will BLAST the ROCK away.
Ready?
Aim...

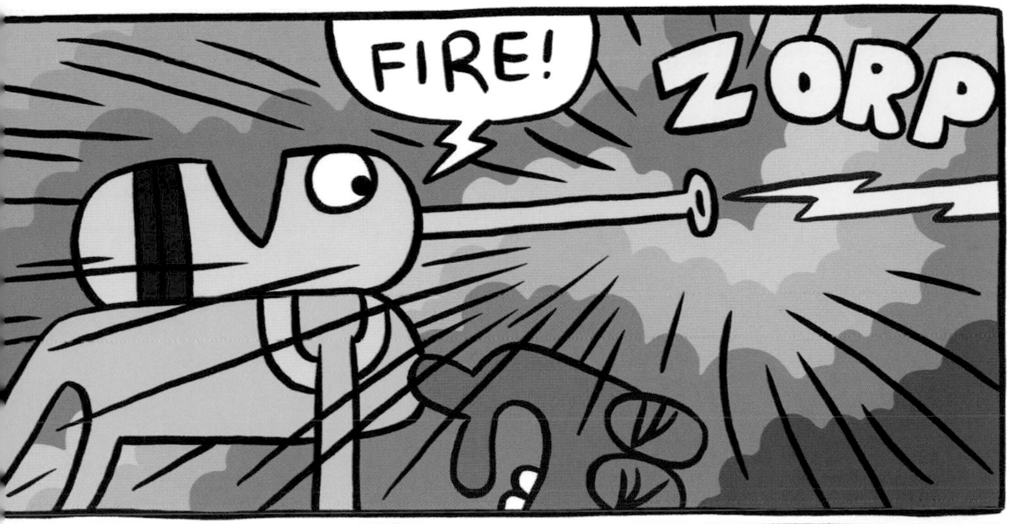
FIRE!
ZORP

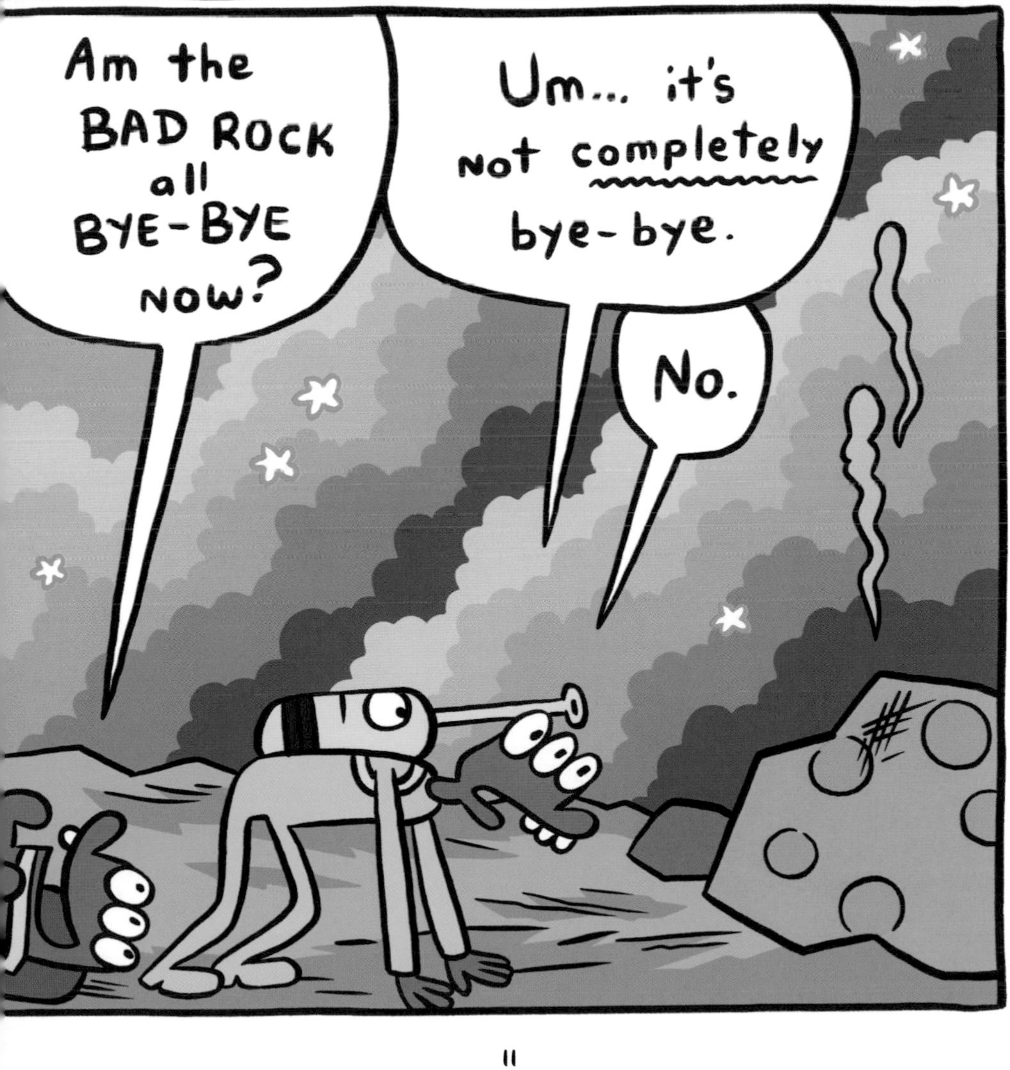
Am the BAD ROCK all BYE-BYE now?
Um... it's not completely bye-bye.
No.

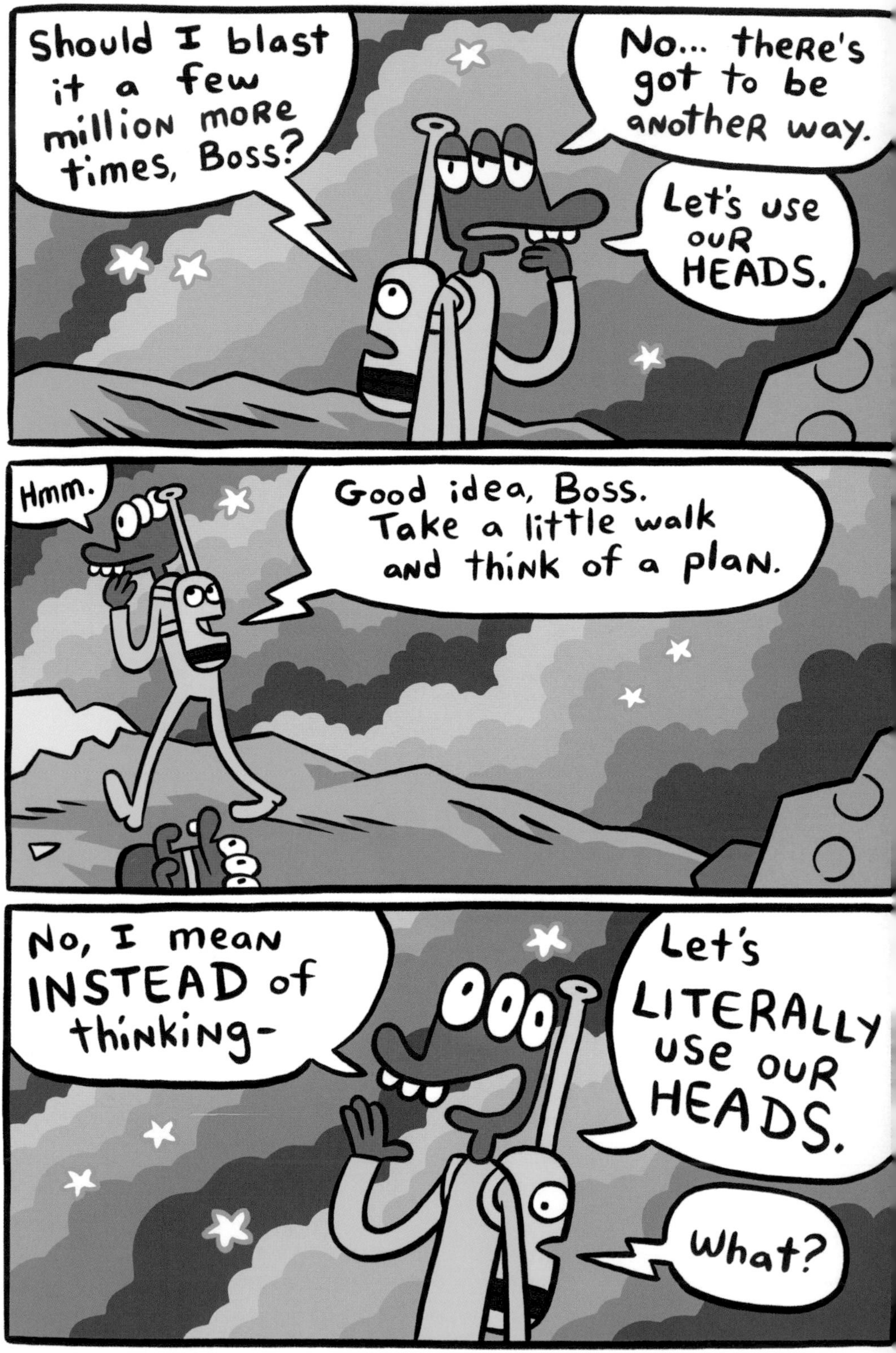
Should I blast it a few million more times, Boss?
No... there's got to be another way.
Let's use our HEADS.
Hmm.
Good idea, Boss. Take a little walk and think of a plan.
No, I mean INSTEAD of thinking-
Let's LITERALLY use our HEADS.
What?

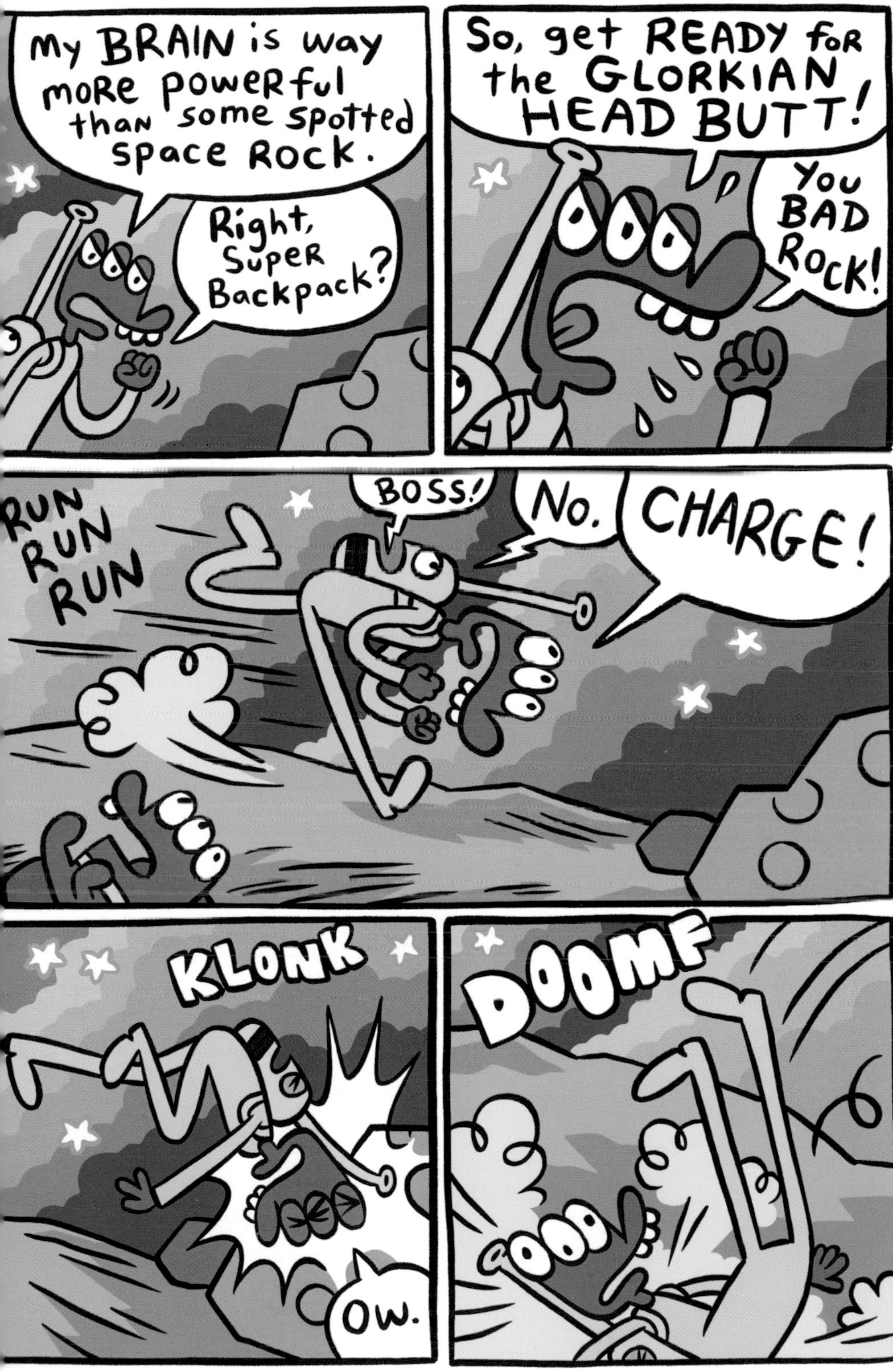
My BRAIN is way more powerful than some spotted space ROCK.
Right, Super Backpack?
So, get READY for the GLORKIAN HEAD BUTT!
You BAD ROCK!
RUN RUN RUN
BOSS!
No.
CHARGE!
KLONK
OW.
DOOMF

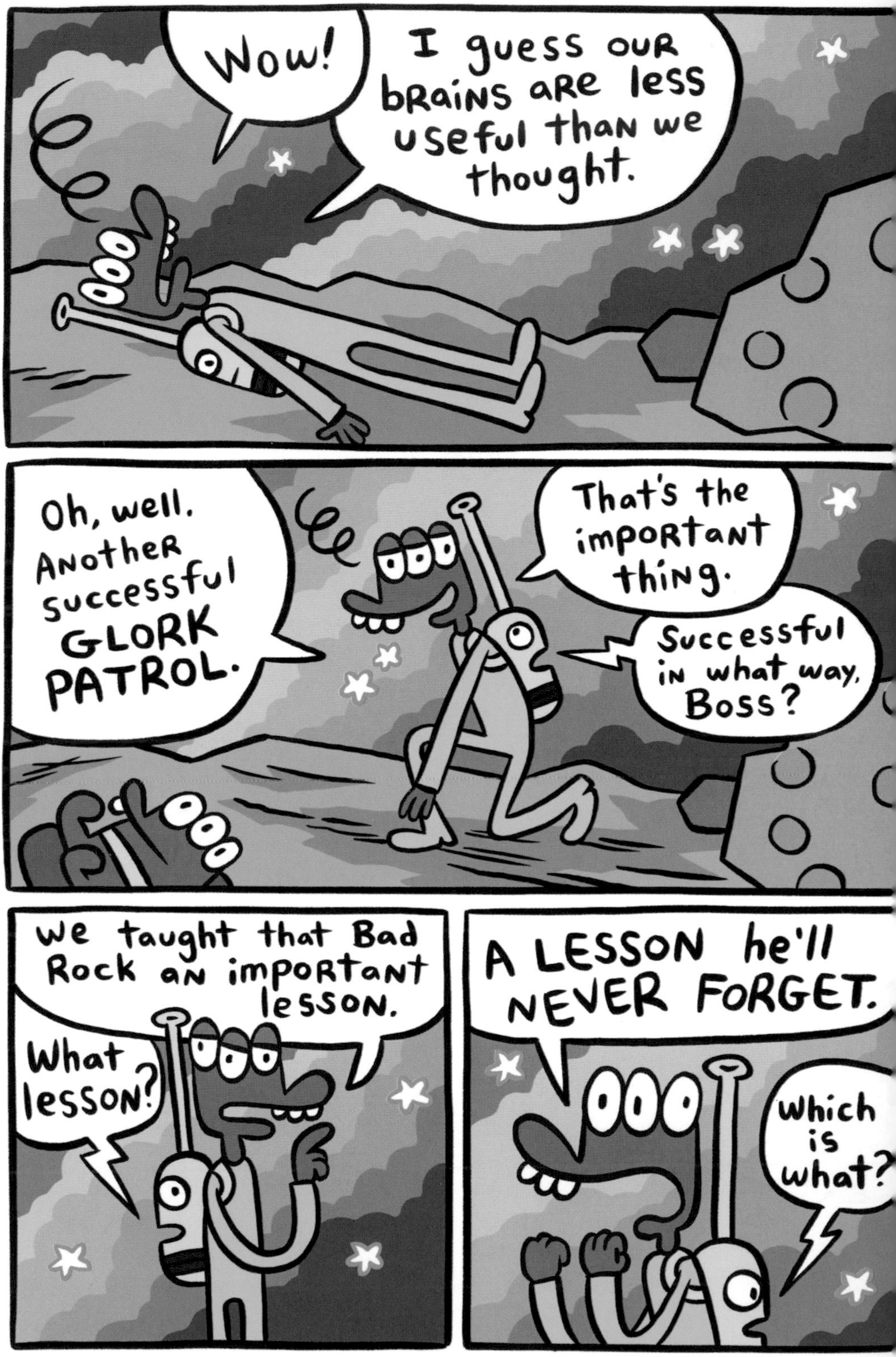
Wow!
I guess our brains are less useful than we thought.
Oh, well. Another successful GLORK PATROL.
That's the important thing.
Successful in what way, Boss?
We taught that Bad Rock an important lesson.
What lesson?
A LESSON he'll NEVER FORGET.
Which is what?

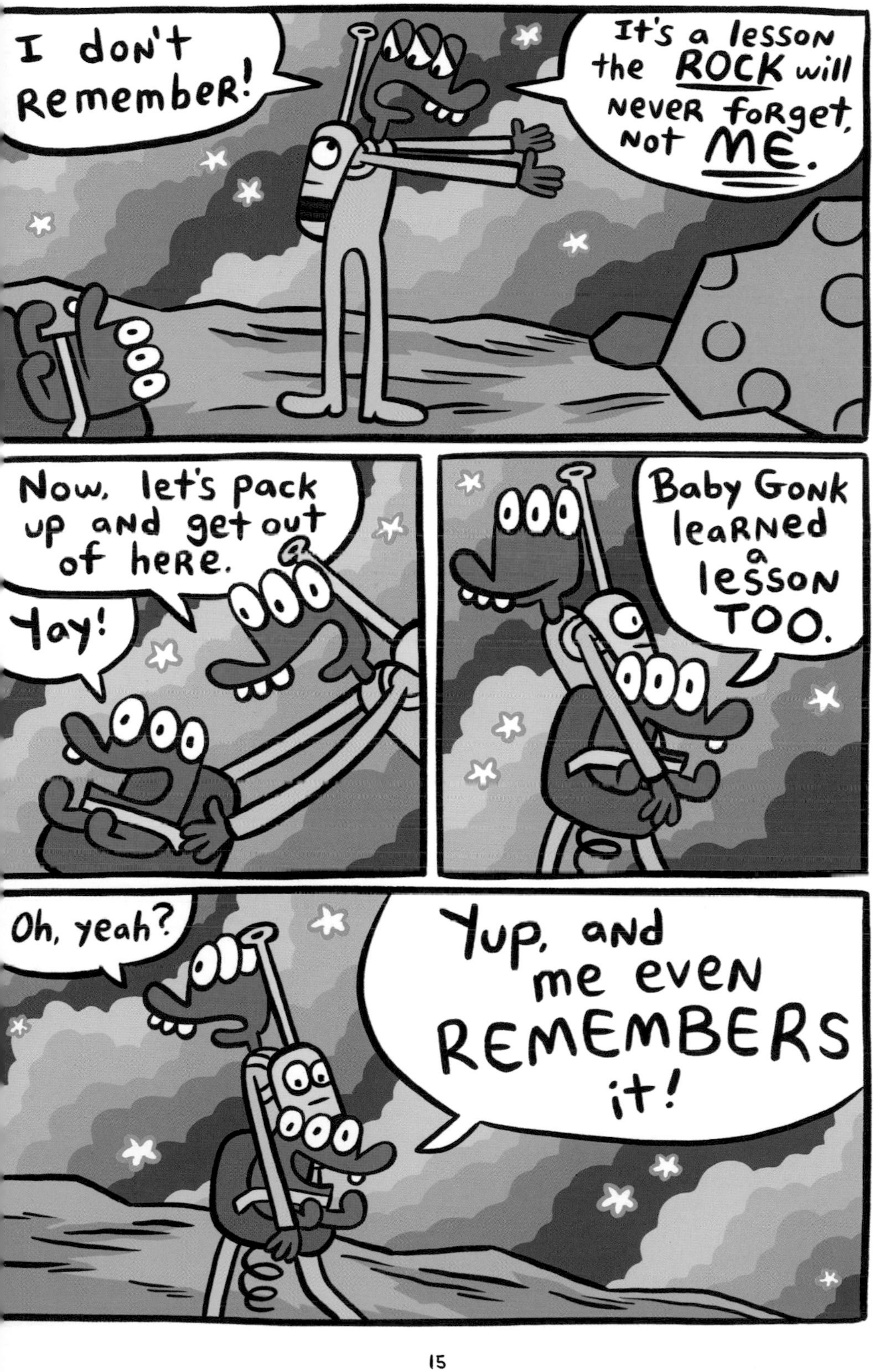
I don't remember!
It's a lesson the ROCK will never forget, not ME.
Now, let's pack up and get out of here.
Yay!
Baby Gonk learned a lesson TOO.
Oh, yeah?
Yup, and me even REMEMBERS it!

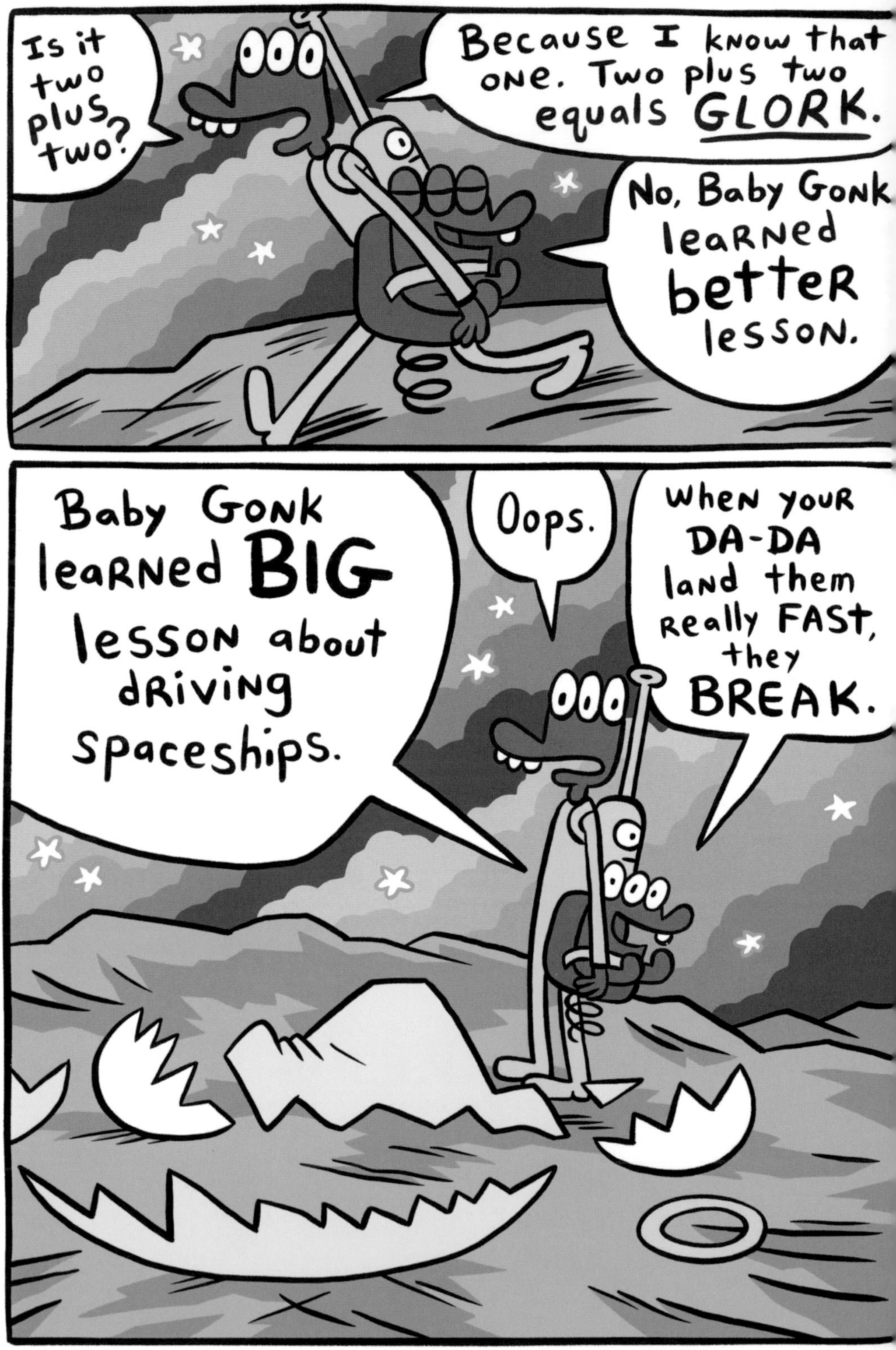
Is it two plus two?
Because I know that one. Two plus two equals GLORK.
No, Baby Gonk learned better lesson.
Baby Gonk learned BIG lesson about driving spaceships.
Oops.
When your DA-DA land them really FAST, they BREAK.

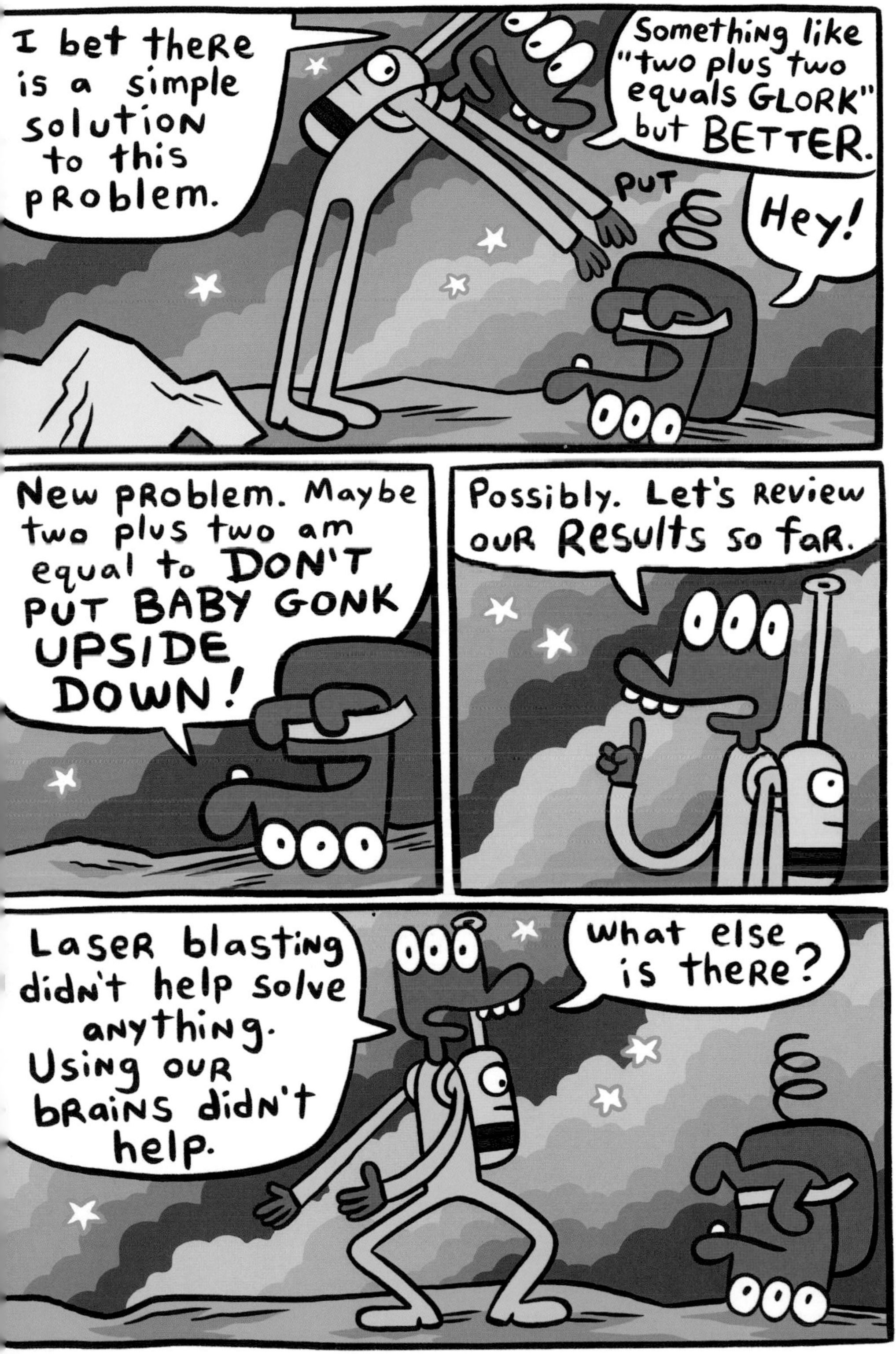
I bet there is a simple solution to this problem.
Something like "two plus two equals GLORK" but BETTER.
PUT
Hey!
New problem. Maybe two plus two am equal to DON'T PUT BABY GONK UPSIDE DOWN!
Possibly. Let's review our results so far.
Laser blasting didn't help solve anything. Using our brains didn't help.
What else is there?

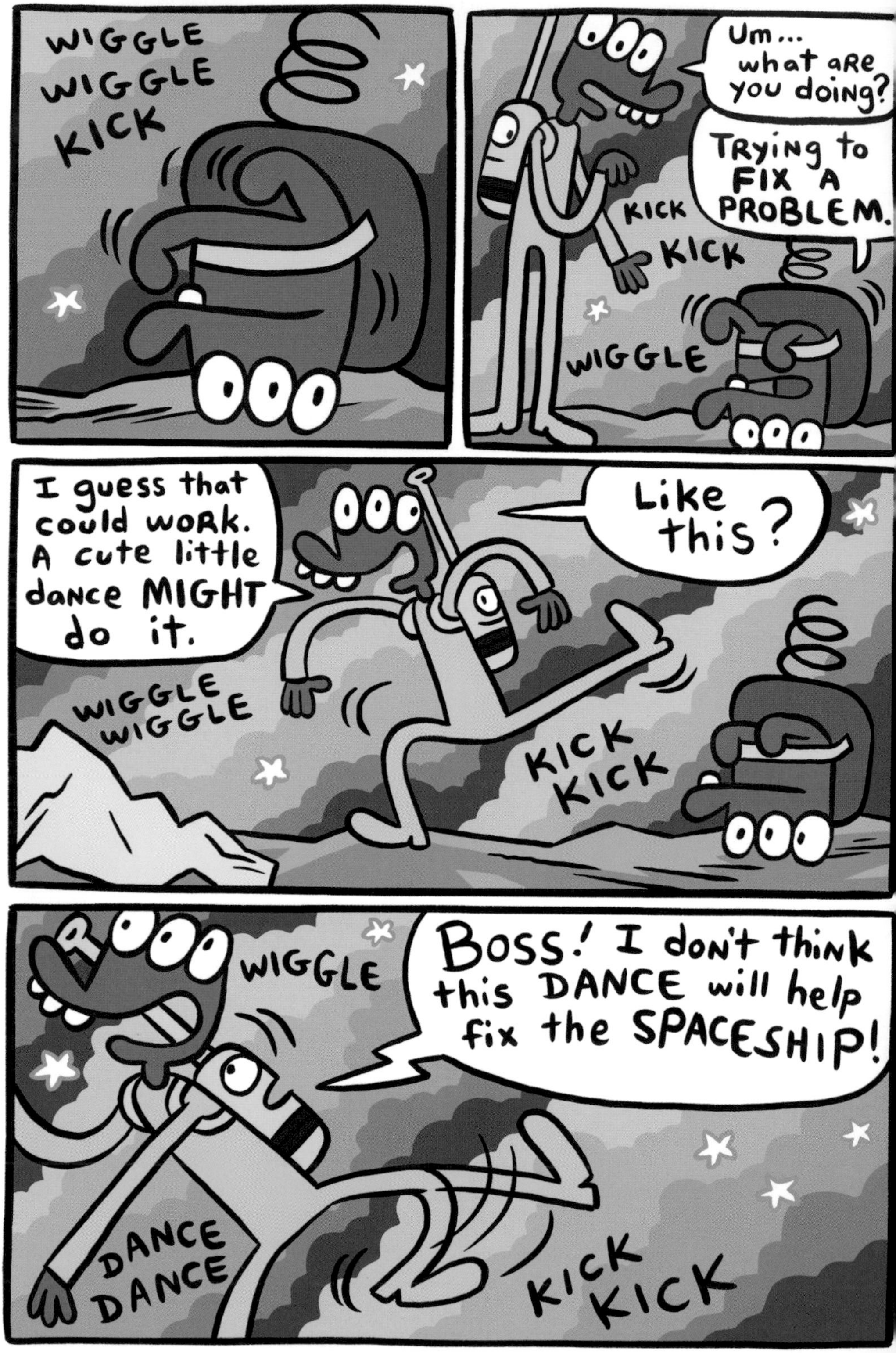
WIGGLE
WIGGLE
KICK
Um... what are you doing?
Trying to FIX A PROBLEM.
KICK
KICK
WIGGLE
I guess that could work. A cute little dance MIGHT do it.
Like this?
WIGGLE
WIGGLE
KICK
KICK
Boss! I don't think this DANCE will help fix the SPACESHIP!
WIGGLE
DANCE
DANCE
KICK
KICK

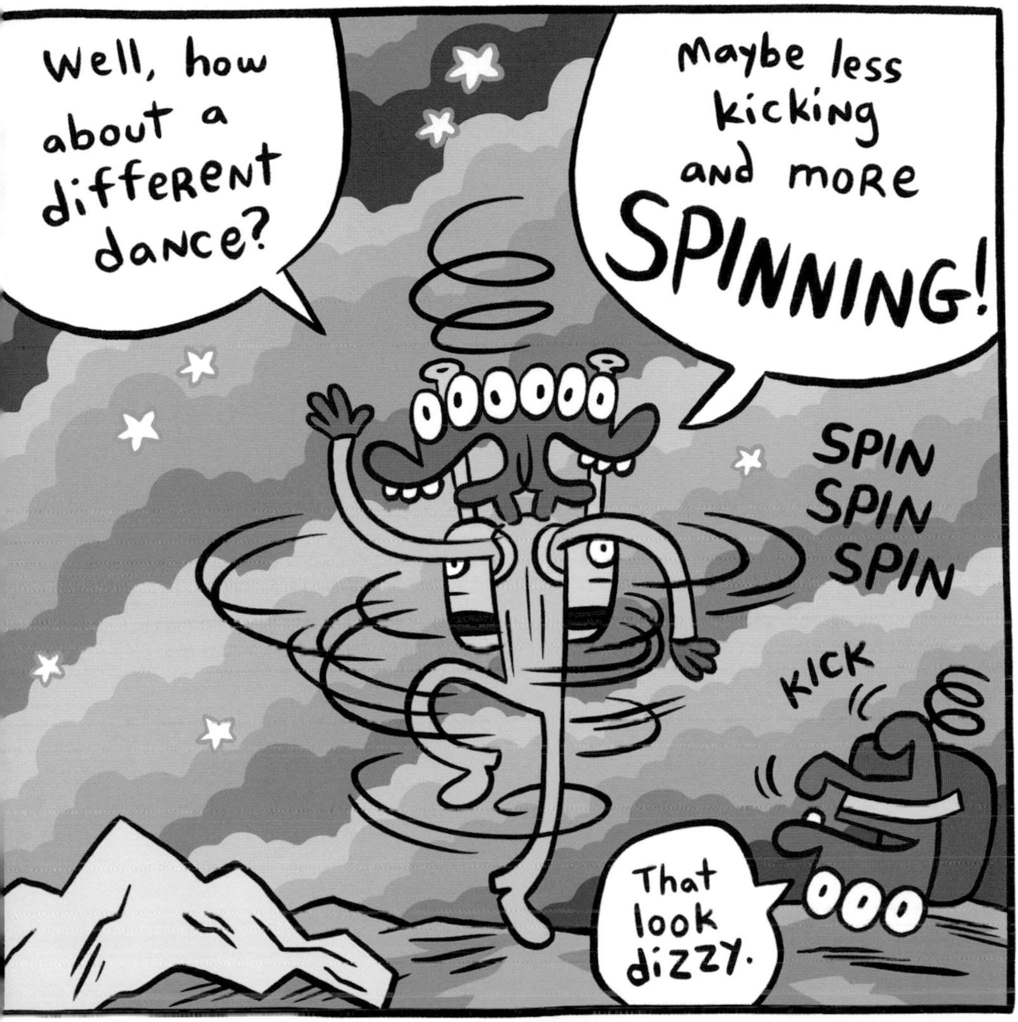
Well, how about a different dance?
Maybe less kicking and more SPINNING!
SPIN SPIN SPIN
KICK
That look dizzy.

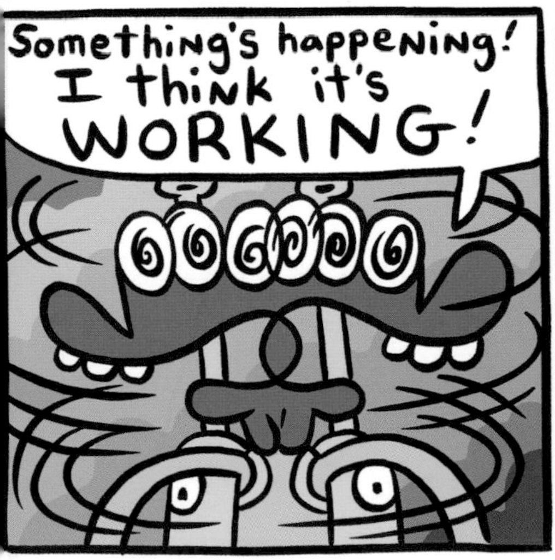
Something's happening! I think it's WORKING!

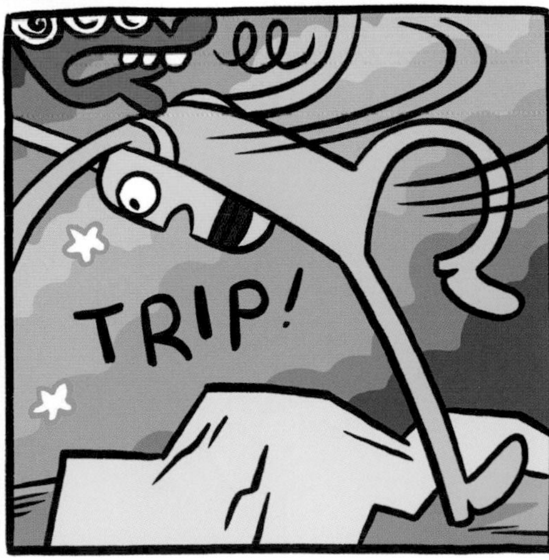
TRIP!

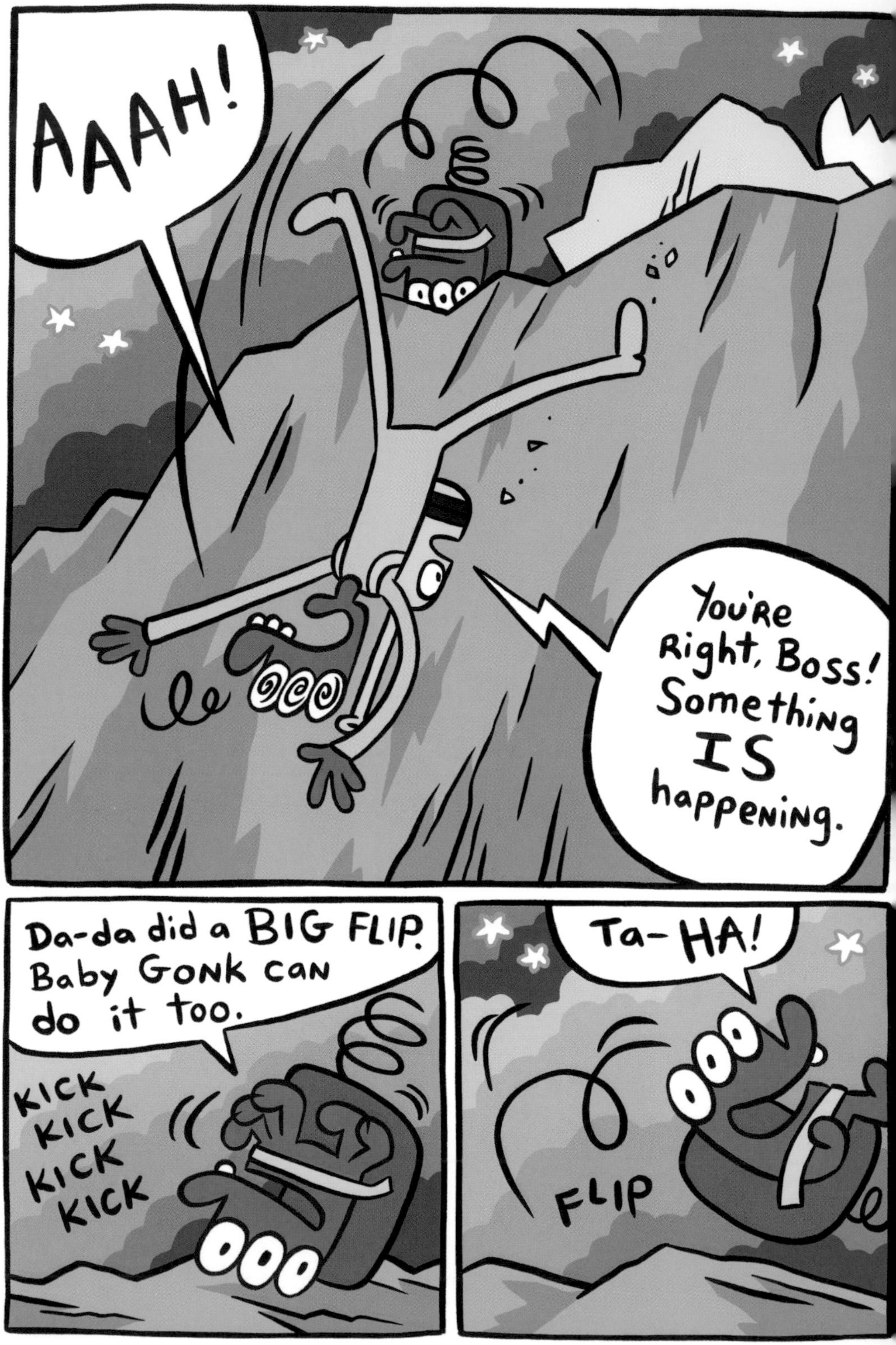
AAAH!
You're Right, Boss! Something IS happening.
Da-da did a BIG FLIP. Baby GONK can do it too.
KICK KICK KICK KICK
Ta-HA!
FLIP

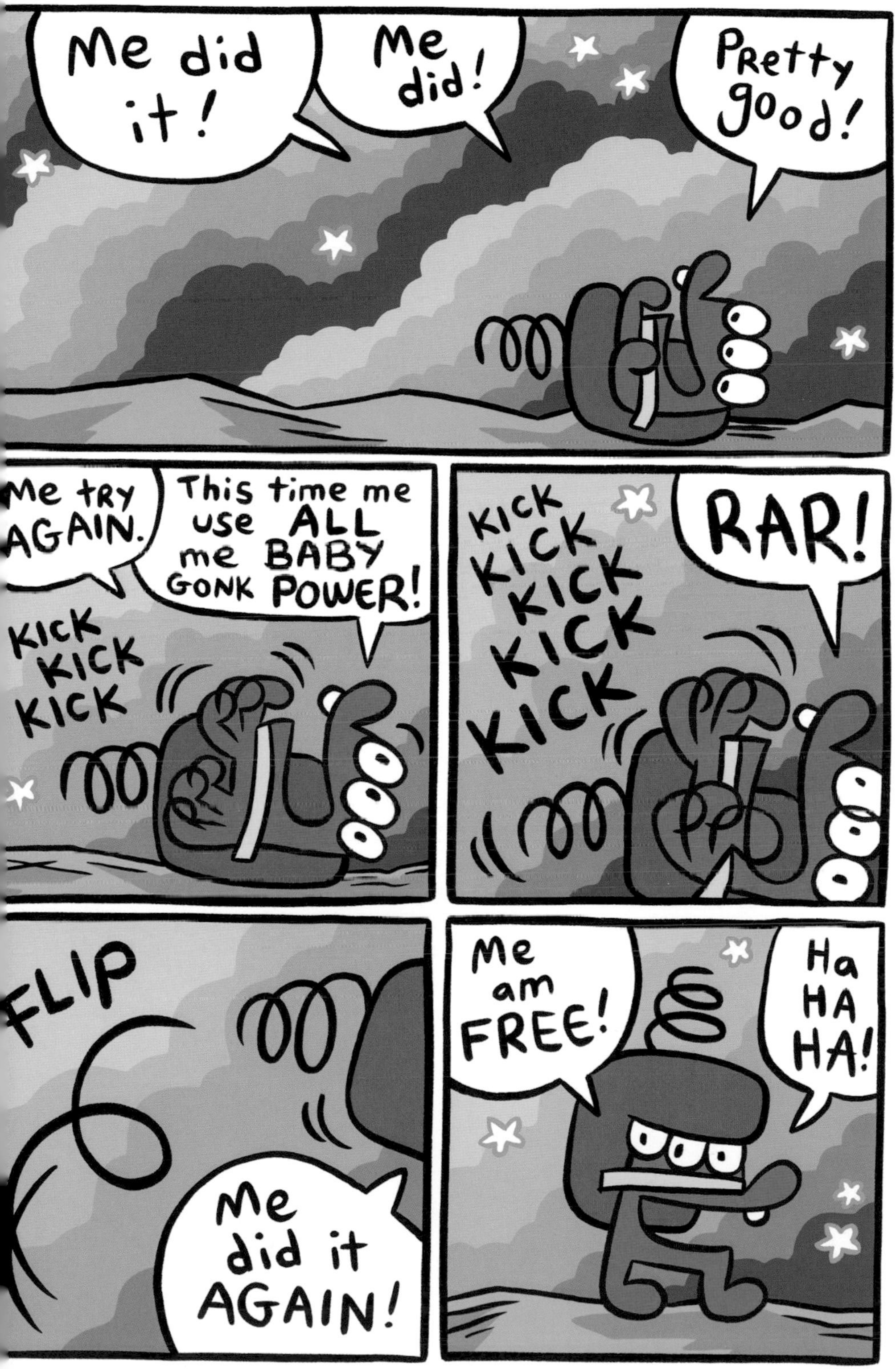

Me did it!
Me did!
Pretty good!
Me try AGAIN.
This time me use ALL me BABY GONK POWER!
KICK KICK KICK
KICK KICK KICK KICK KICK
RAR!
FLIP
Me did it AGAIN!
Me am FREE!
Ha HA HA!

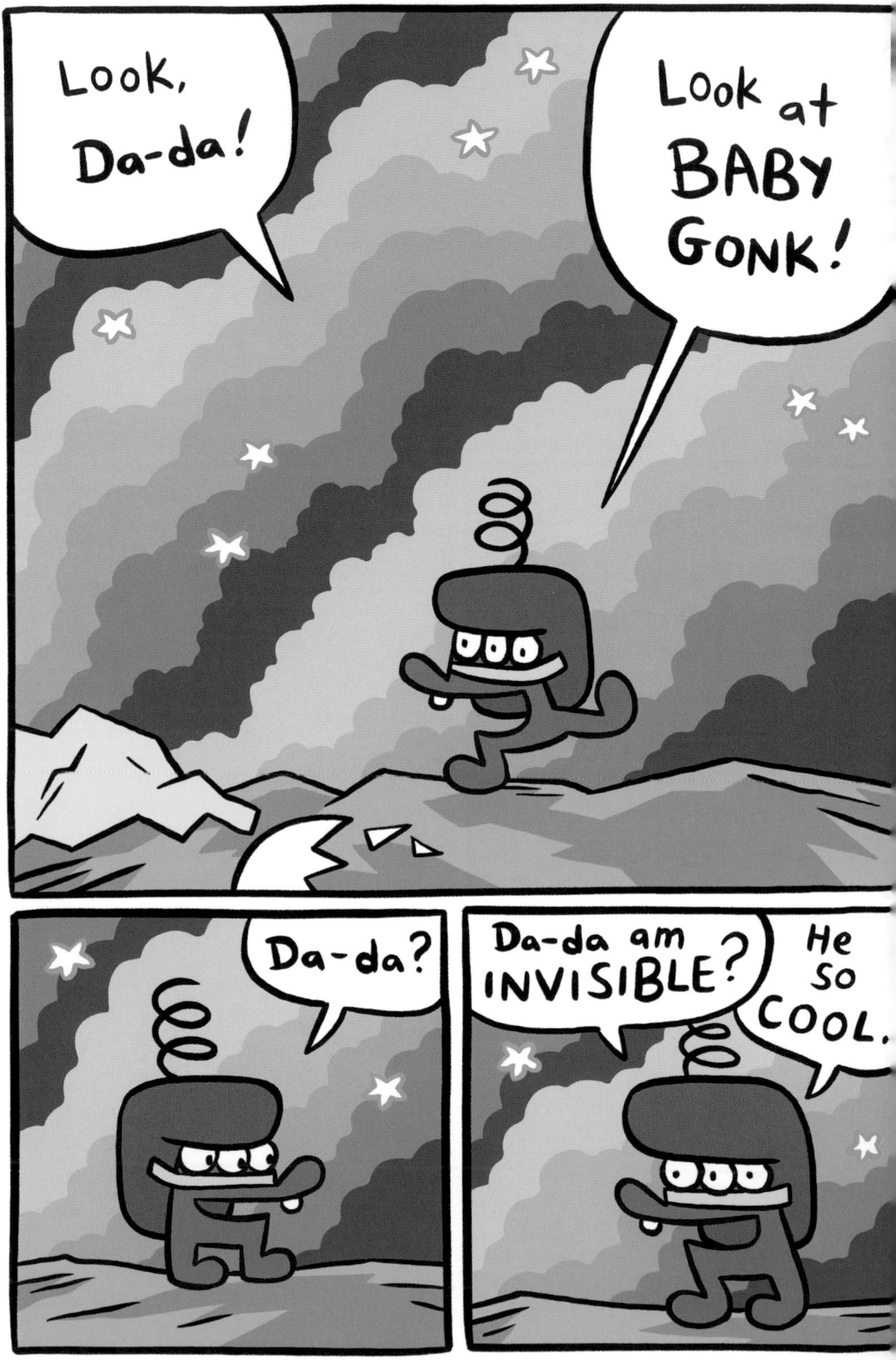
LOOK, Da-da!
LOOK at BABY GONK!
Da-da?
Da-da am INVISIBLE?
He so COOL.

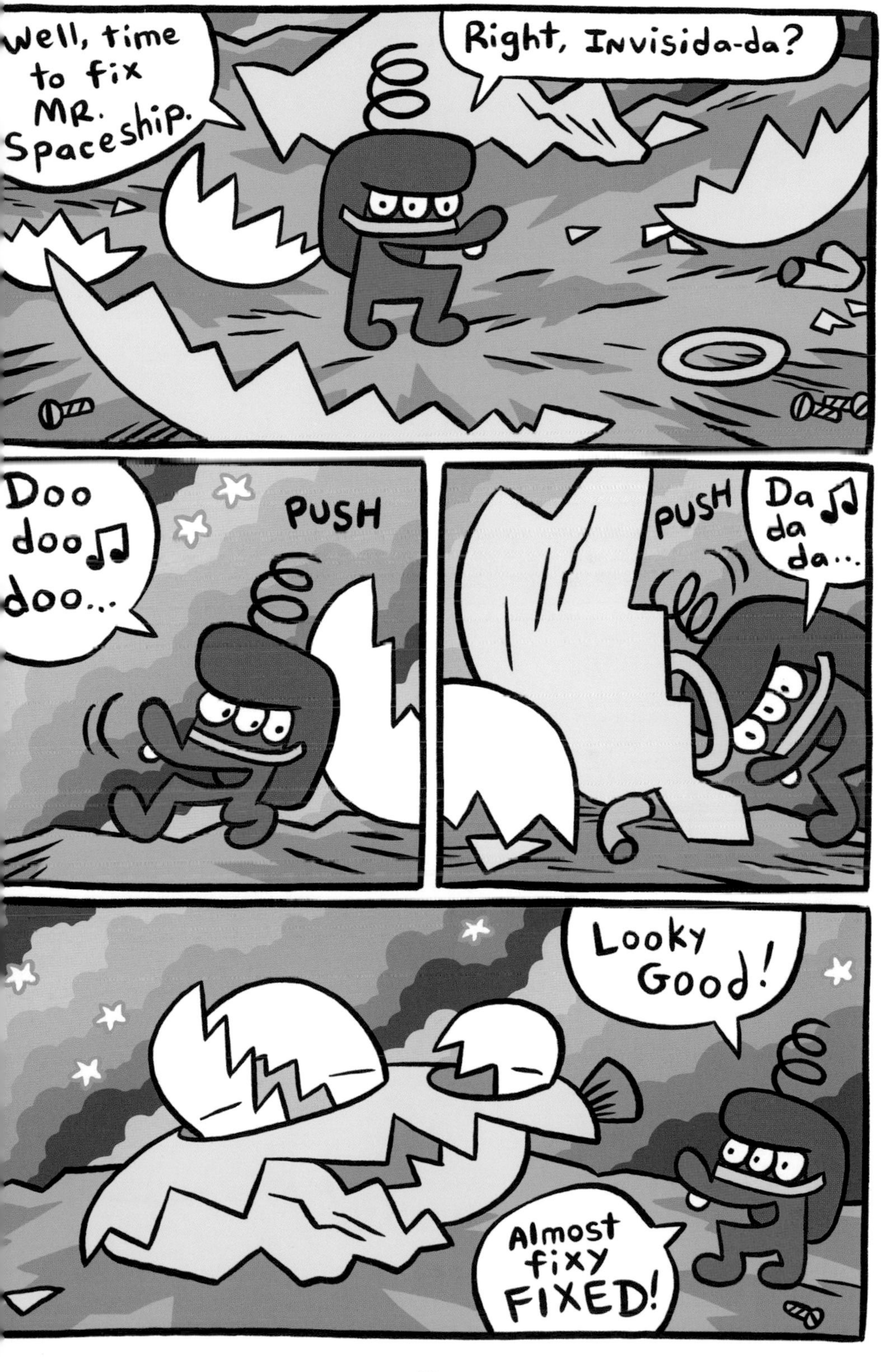
Well, time to fix MR. Spaceship.
Right, INVISIDA-DA?
Doo doo♫ doo...
PUSH
PUSH
Da♫ da da...
Looky Good!
Almost fixy FIXED!

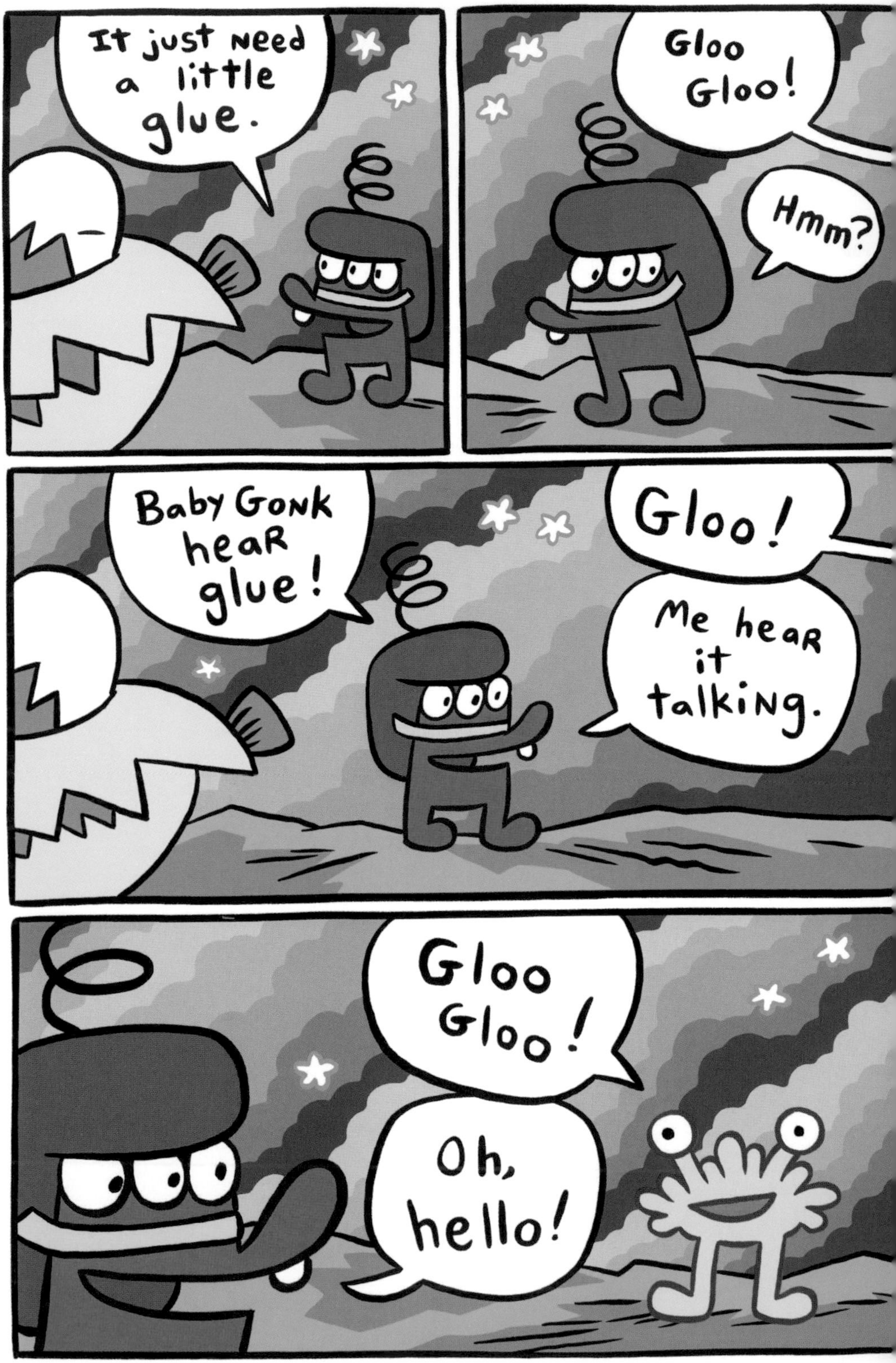
It just need a little glue.
Gloo Gloo!
Hmm?
Baby Gonk hear glue!
Gloo!
Me hear it talking.
Gloo Gloo!
Oh, hello!

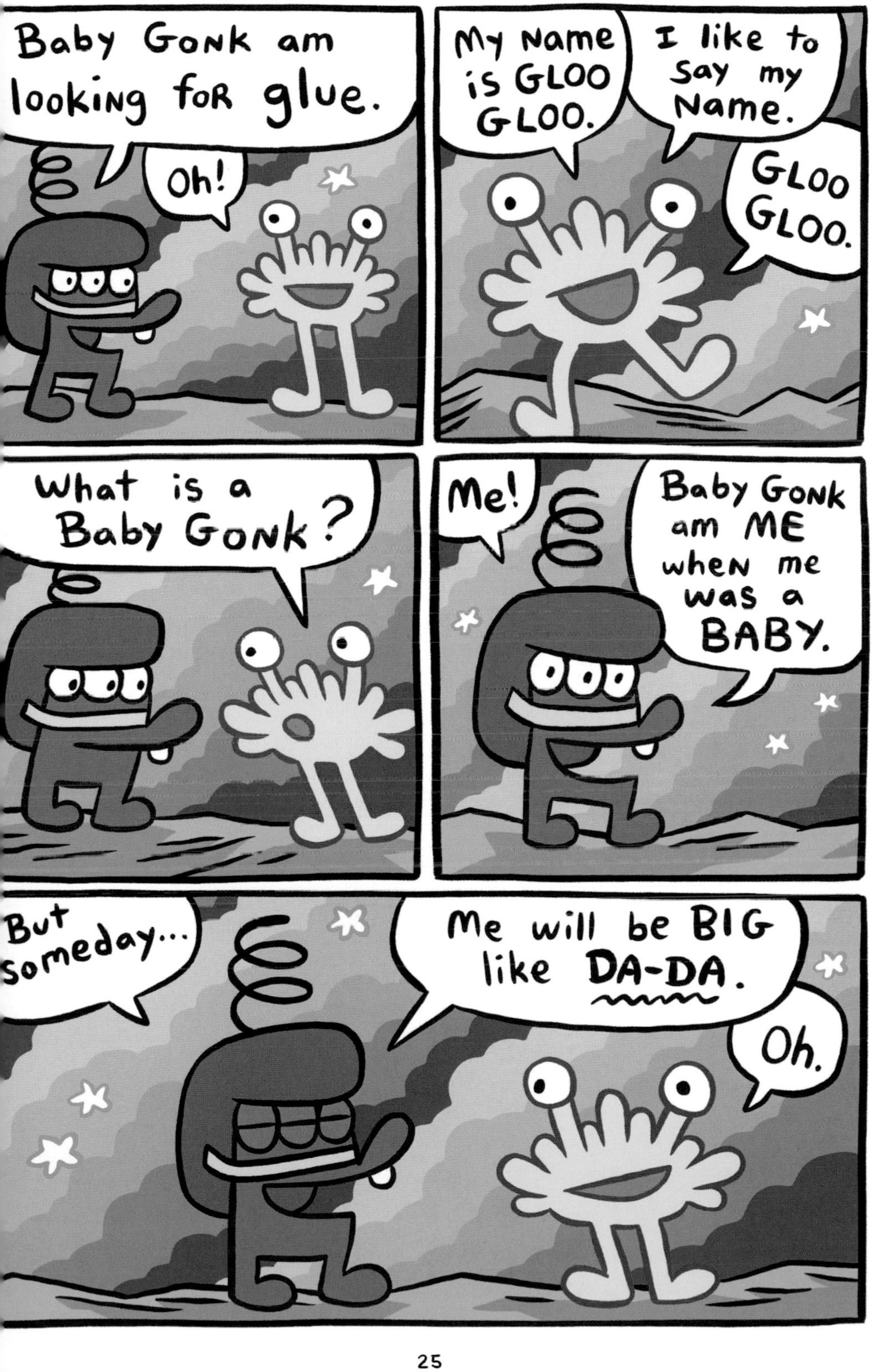
Baby Gonk am looking for glue.
Oh!
My Name is GLOO GLOO.
I like to say my Name.
GLOO GLOO.
What is a Baby Gonk?
Me!
Baby Gonk am ME when me was a BABY.
But someday...
Me will be BIG like DA-DA.
Oh.

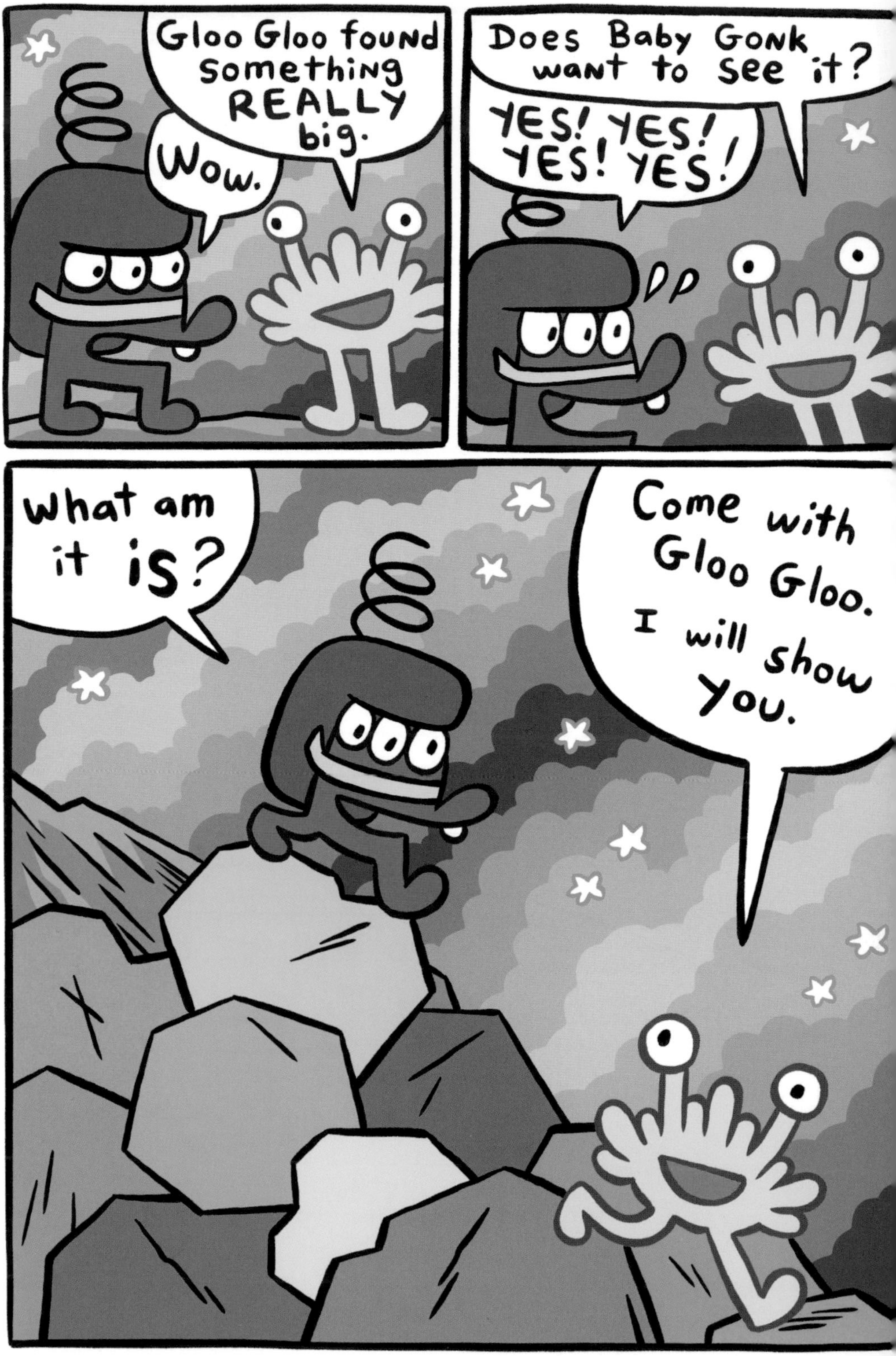
Gloo Gloo found something REALLY big.
Wow.
Does Baby Gonk want to see it?
YES! YES! YES! YES!
What am it is?
Come with Gloo Gloo. I will show you.

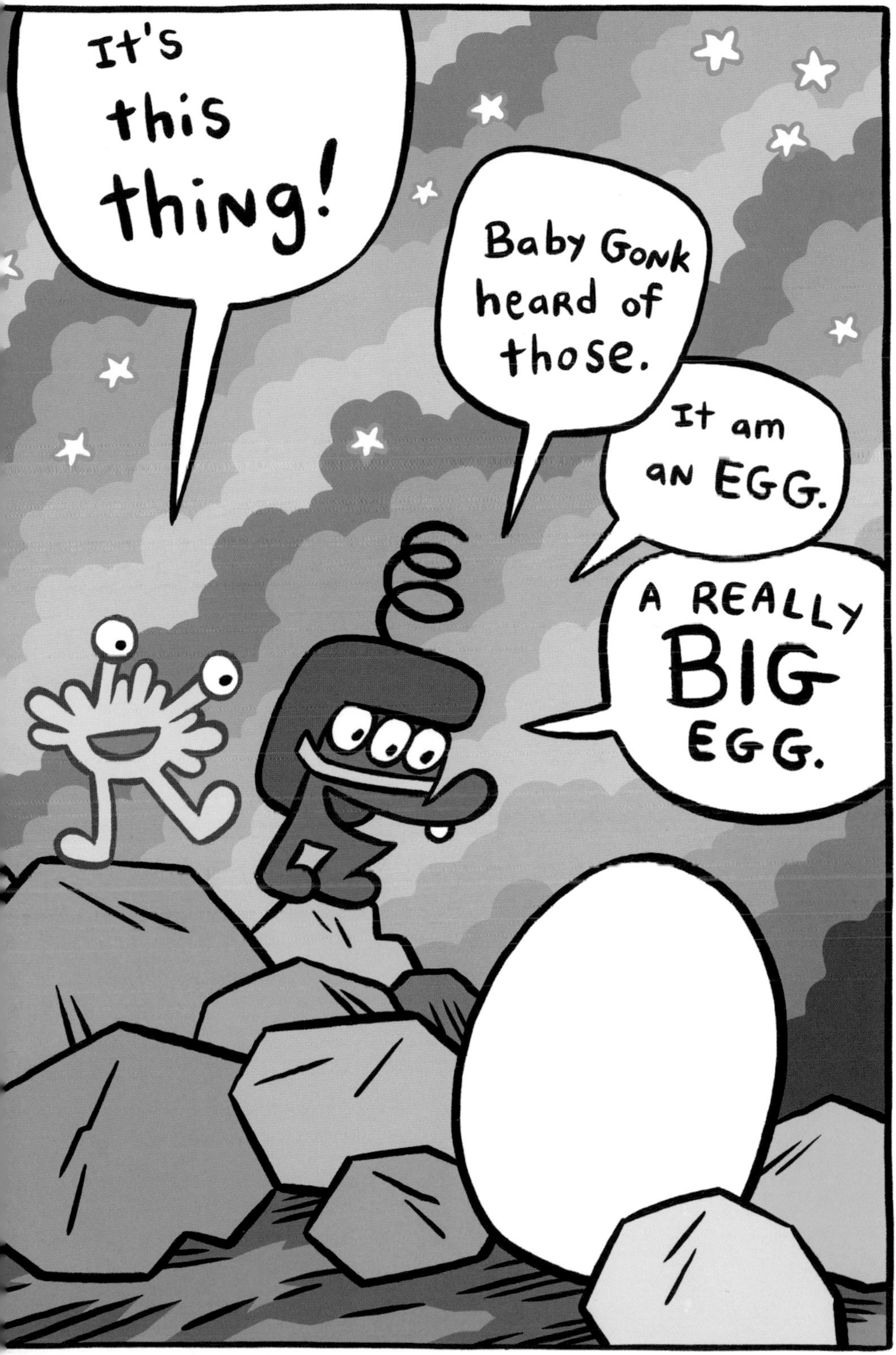
It's this thing!
Baby Gonk heard of those.
It am an EGG.
A REALLY BIG EGG.

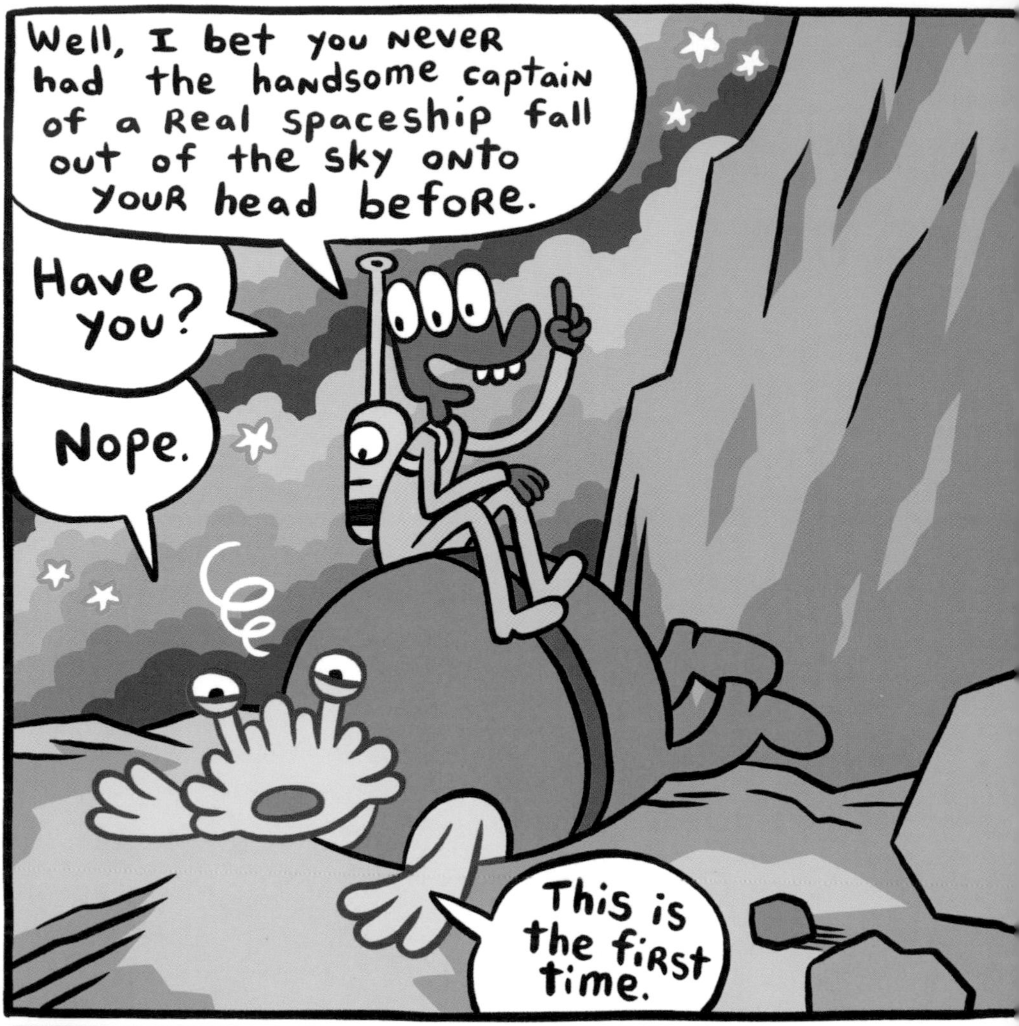
Well, I bet you never had the handsome captain of a real spaceship fall out of the sky onto your head before.
Have you?
Nope.
This is the first time.

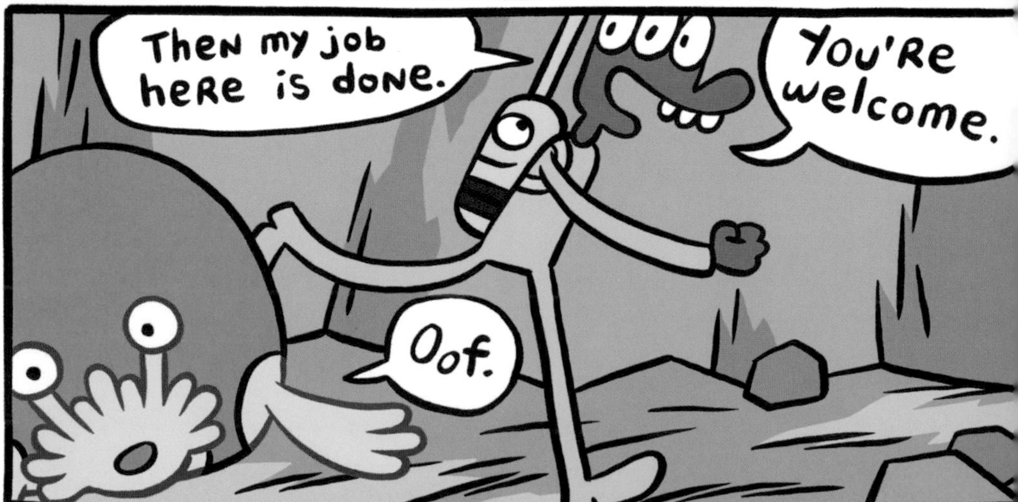
Then my job here is done.
You're welcome.
Oof.

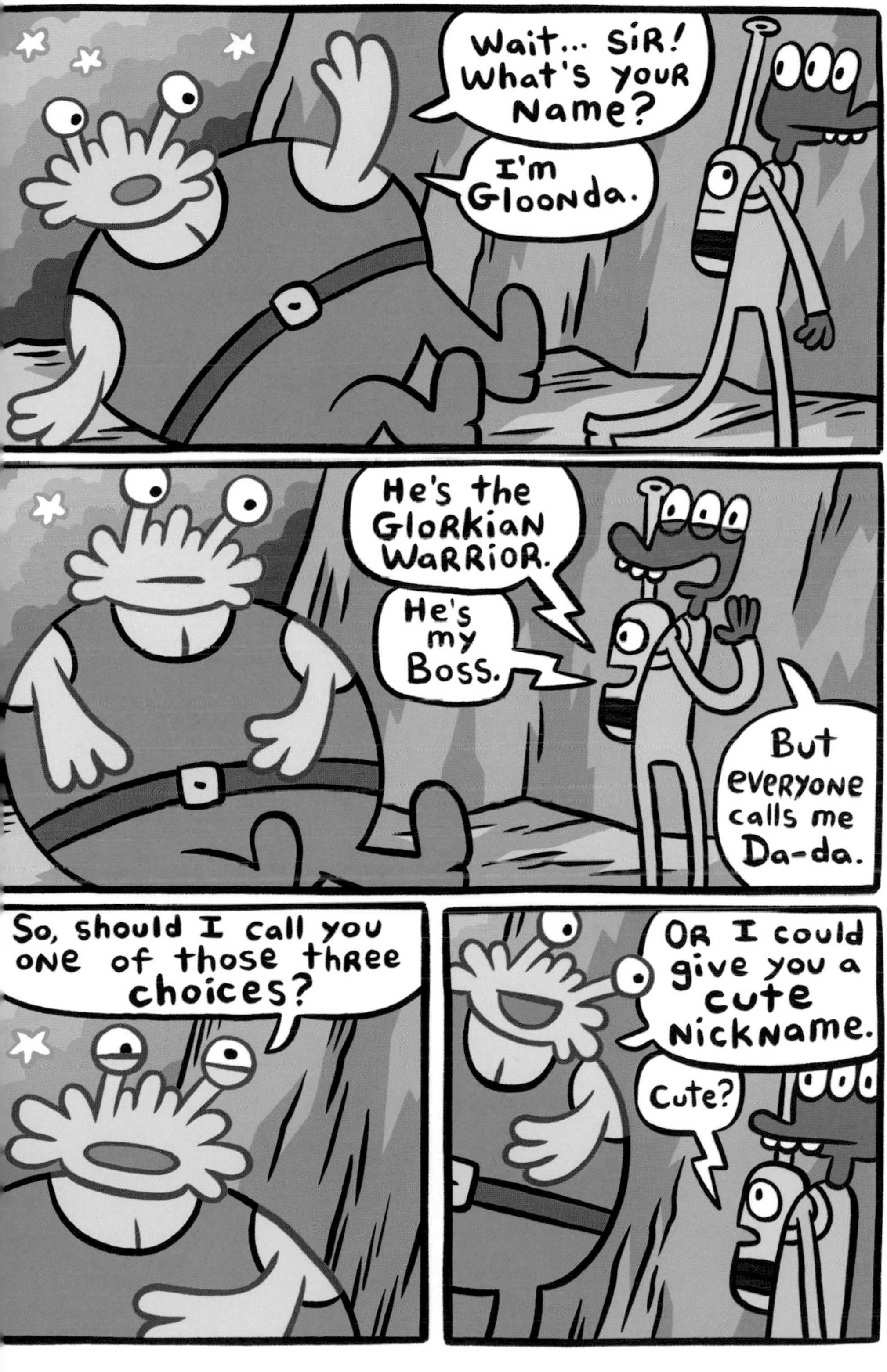
Wait... SIR! What's YOUR Name?
I'm Gloonda.
He's the GLORKIAN WARRIOR.
He's my Boss.
But everyone calls me Da-da.
So, should I call you one of those three choices?
OR I could give you a cute nickname.
Cute?

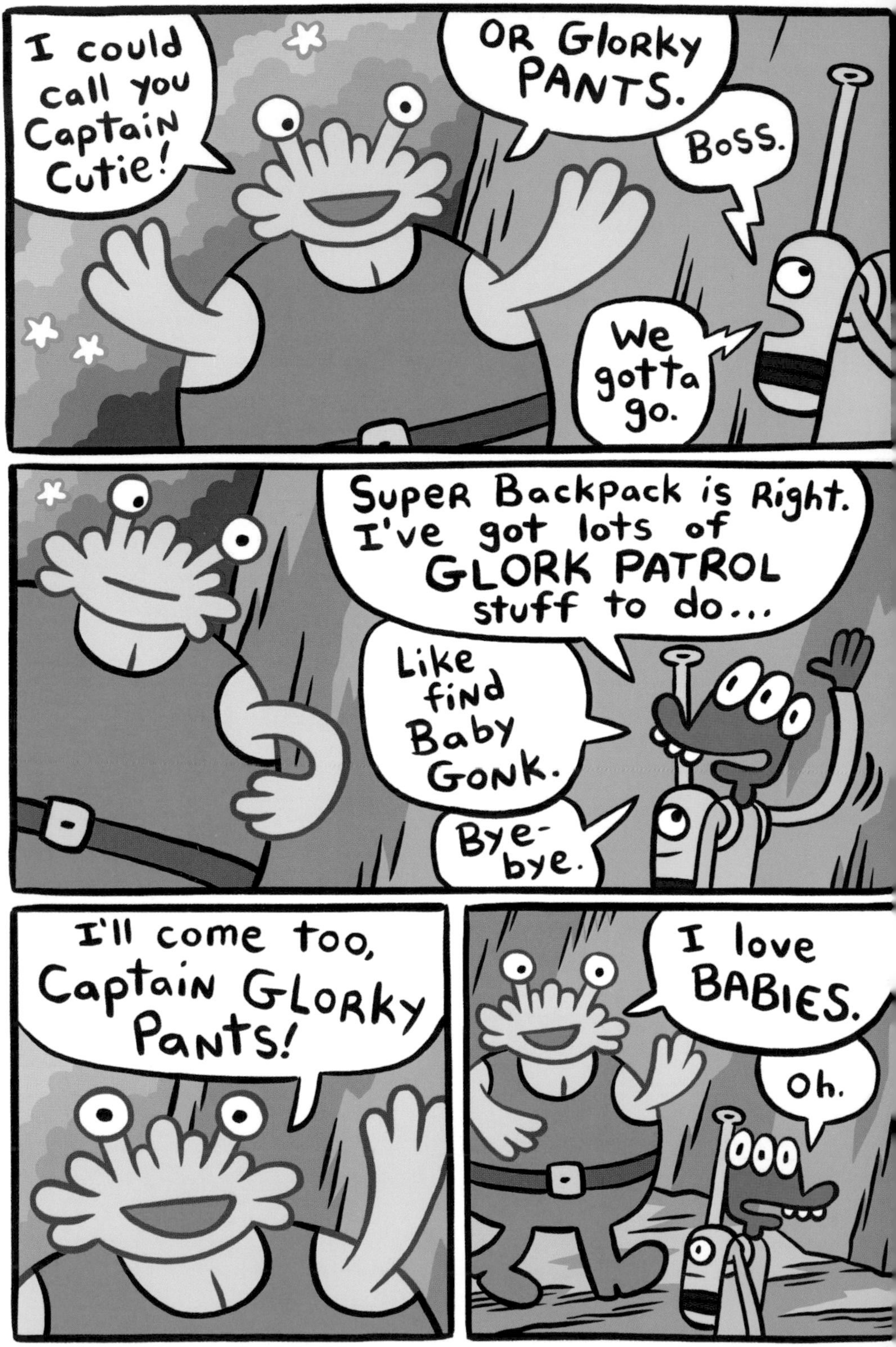
I could call you Captain Cutie!
OR Glorky PANTS.
Boss.
We gotta go.
Super Backpack is Right. I've got lots of GLORK PATROL stuff to do...
Like find Baby GONK.
Bye-bye.
I'll come too, Captain GLORKy Pants!
I love BABIES.
Oh.

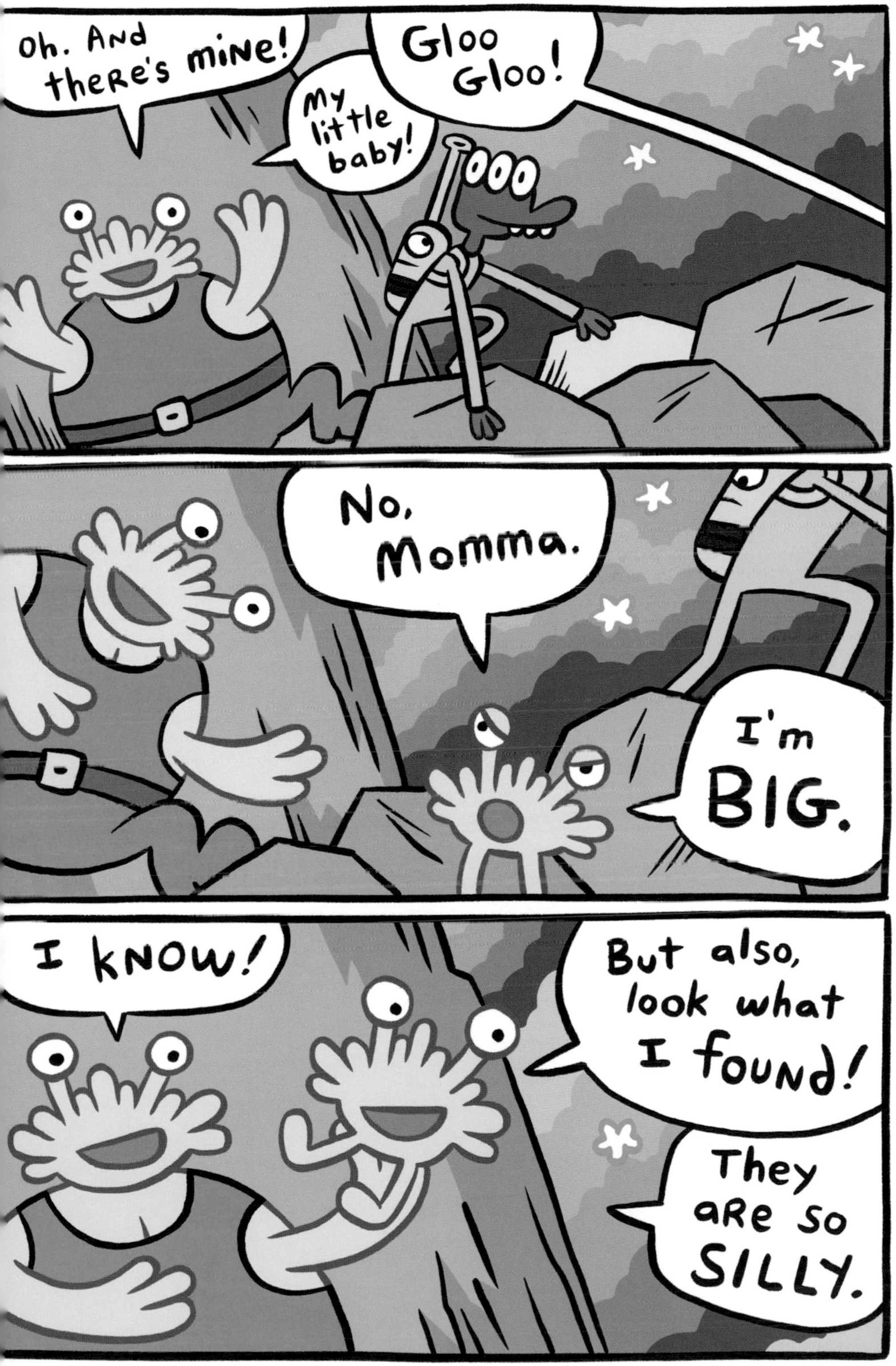
Oh. And there's mine!
My little baby!
Gloo Gloo!
No, Momma.
I'm BIG.
I KNOW!
But also, look what I found!
They are so SILLY.

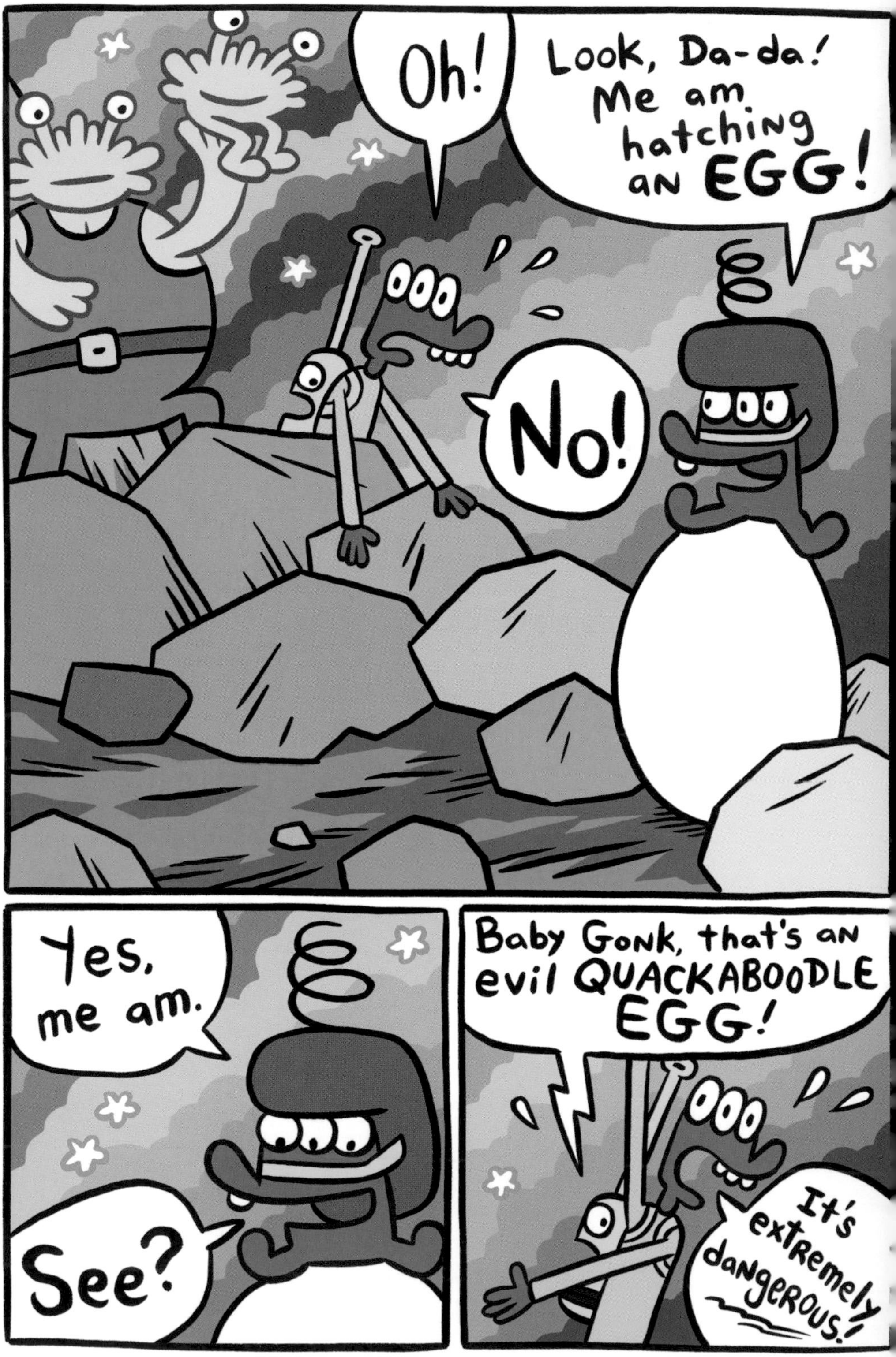
Oh!
Look, Da-da! Me am hatching an EGG!
No!
Yes, me am.
See?
Baby Gonk, that's an evil QUACKABOODLE EGG!
It's extremely dangerous!

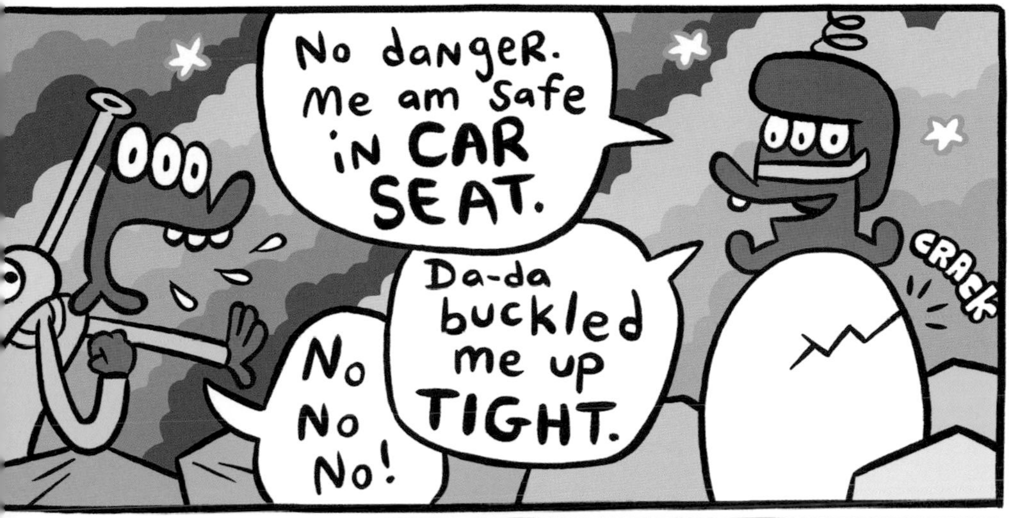
No danger. Me am safe in CAR SEAT.
No No No!
Da-da buckled me up TIGHT.
CRACK

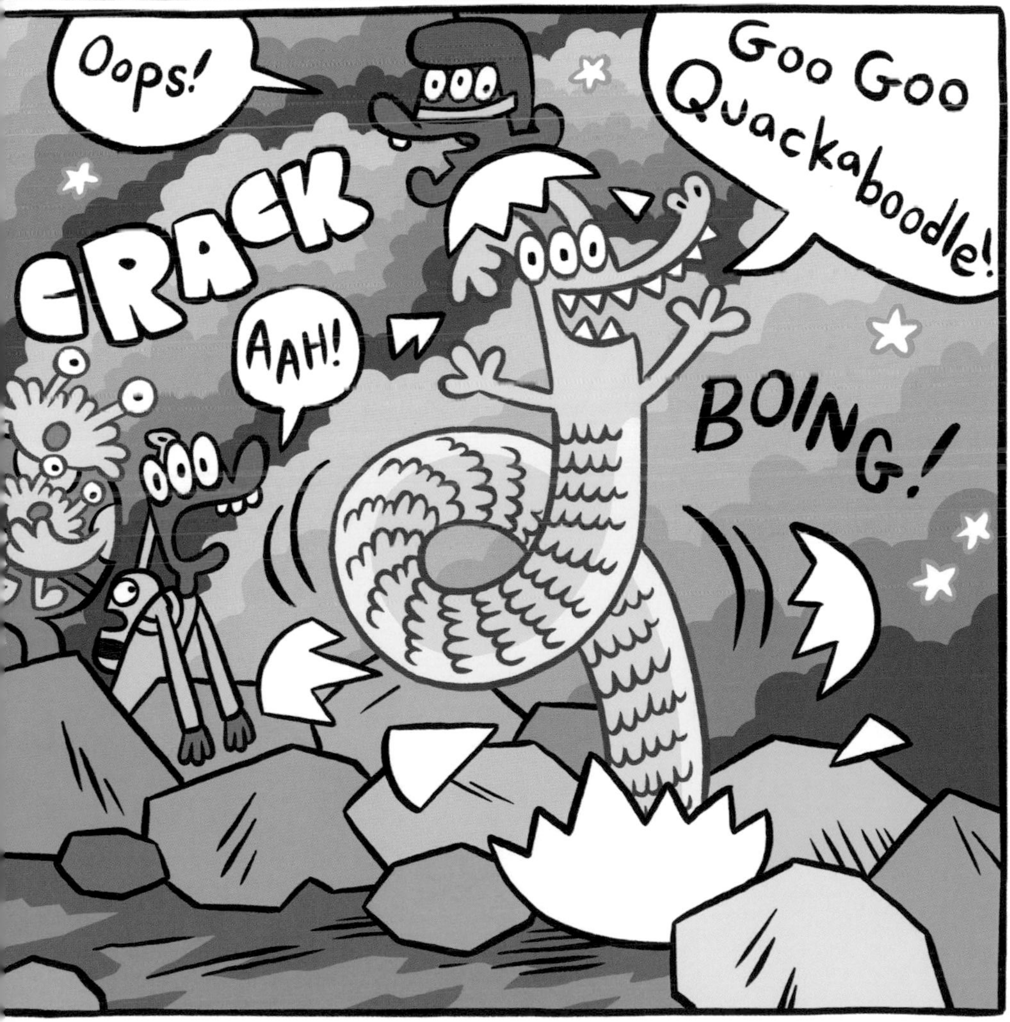
Oops!
Goo Goo Quackaboodle!
CRACK
AAH!
BOING!

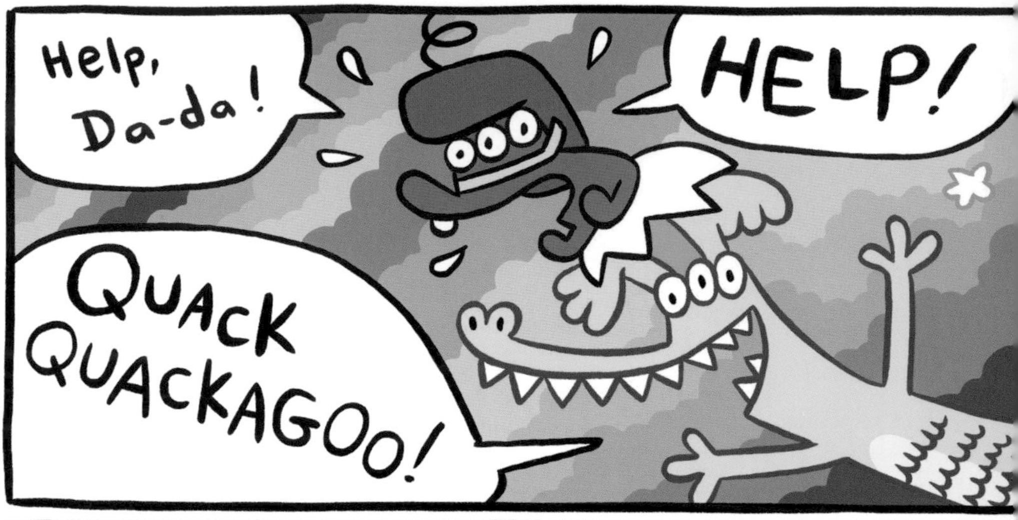
Help, Da-da!
HELP!
QUACK QUACKAGOO!

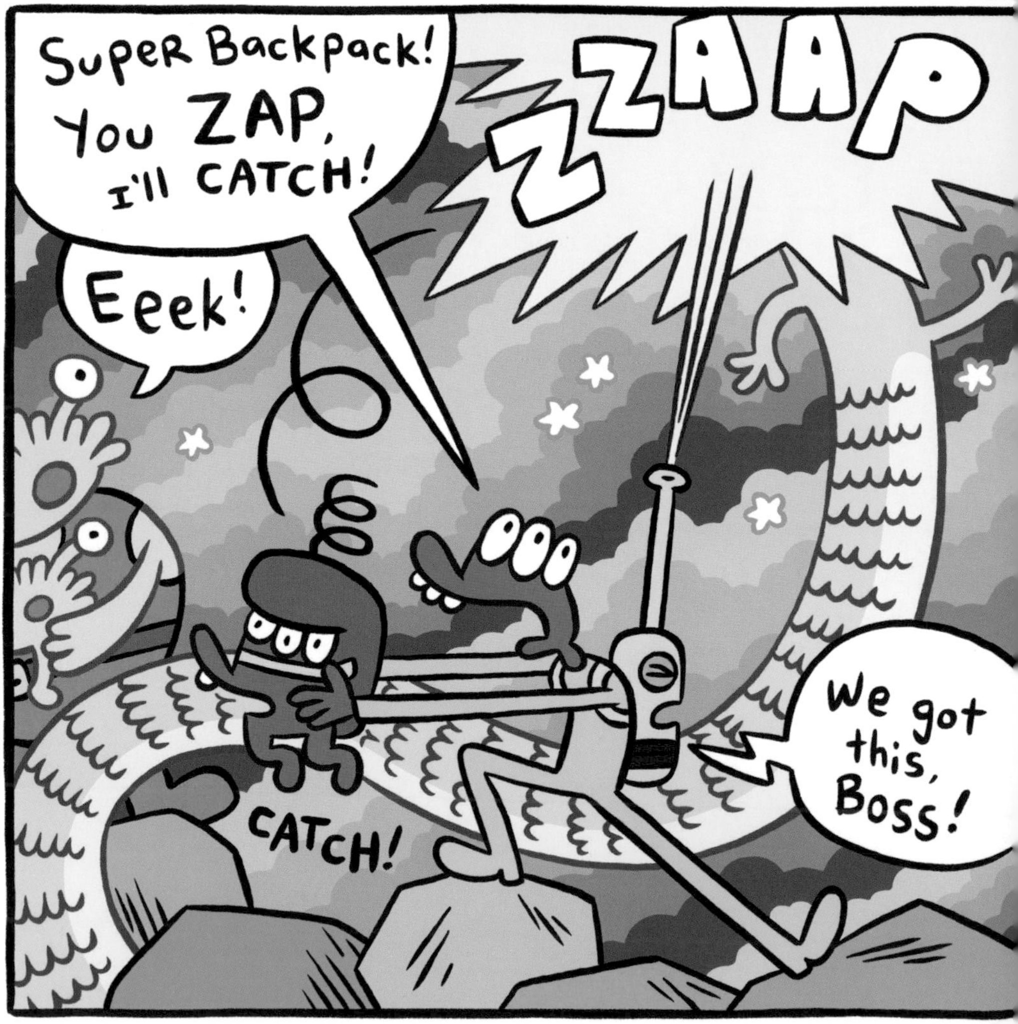
Super Backpack! You ZAP, I'll CATCH!
ZZAAP
Eeek!
We got this, Boss!
CATCH!

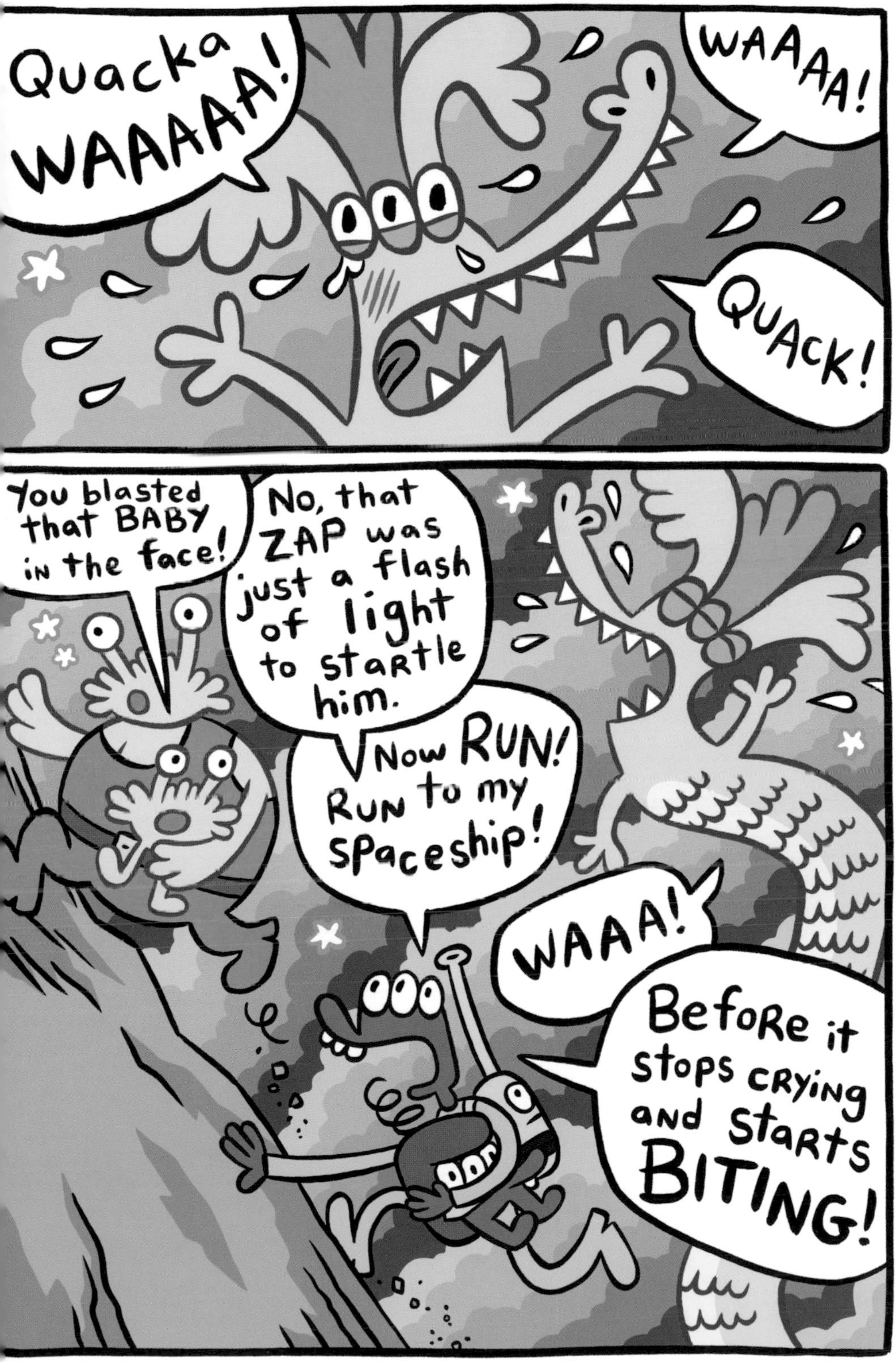
Quacka WAAAAA!
WAAAA!
QUACK!
You blasted that BABY in the face!
No, that ZAP was just a flash of light to startle him.
Now RUN! RUN to my spaceship!
WAAA!
Before it stops crying and starts BITING!

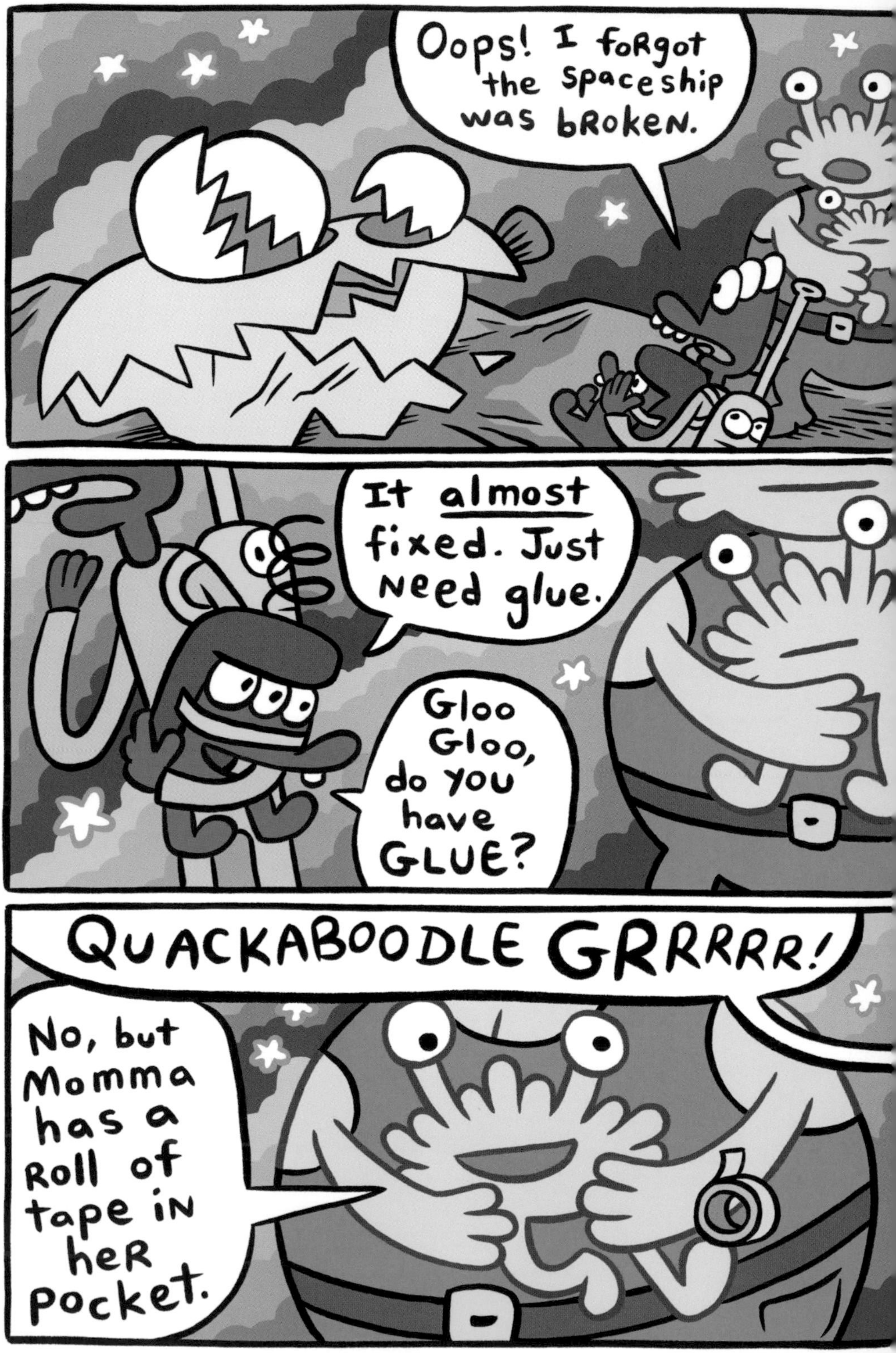
Oops! I forgot the spaceship was broken.
It almost fixed. Just need glue.
Gloo Gloo, do you have GLUE?
QUACKABOODLE GRRRRR!
No, but Momma has a Roll of tape in her pocket.

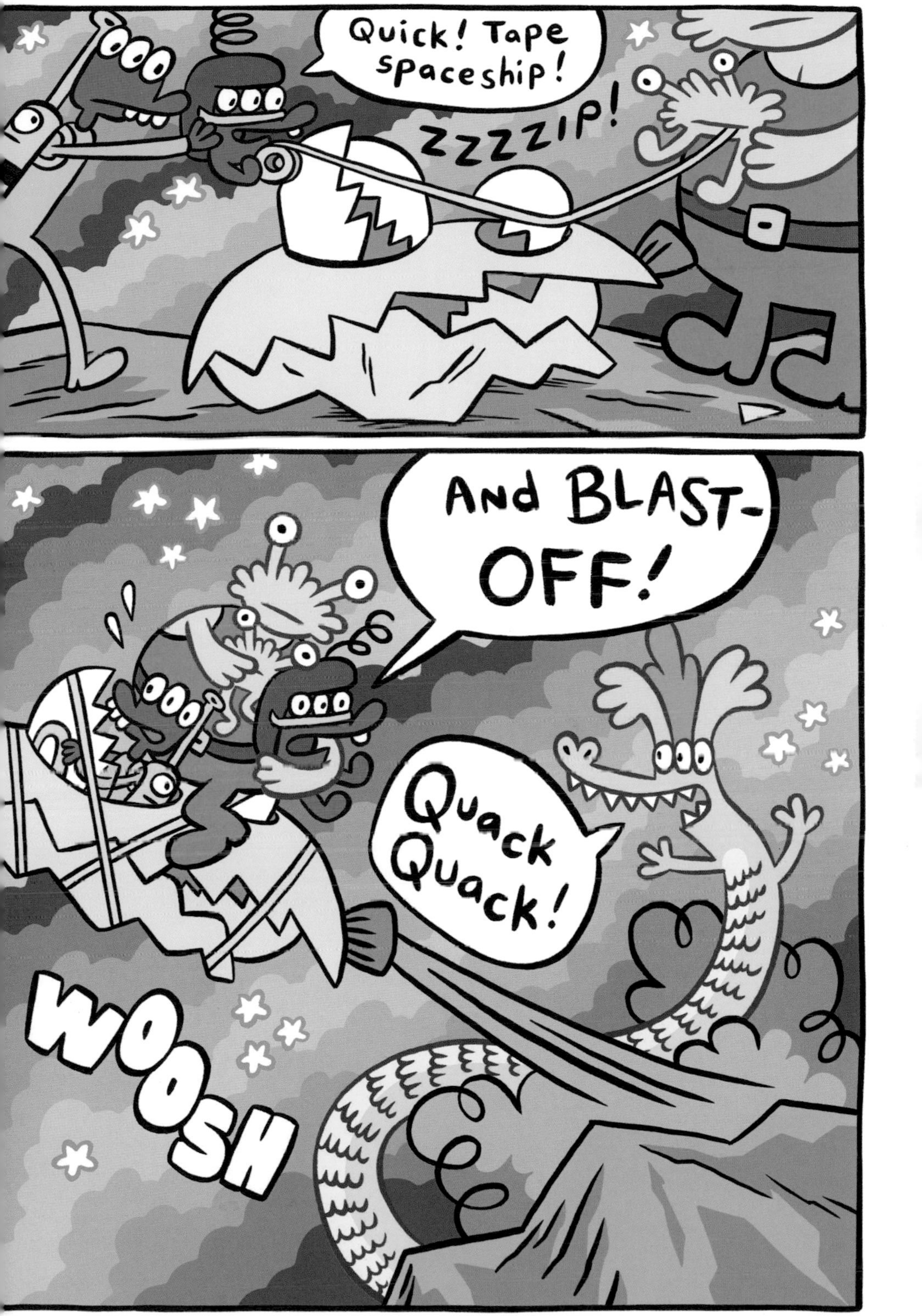
Quick! Tape spaceship!
ZZZZZIP!
AND BLAST-OFF!
Quack Quack!
WOOSH

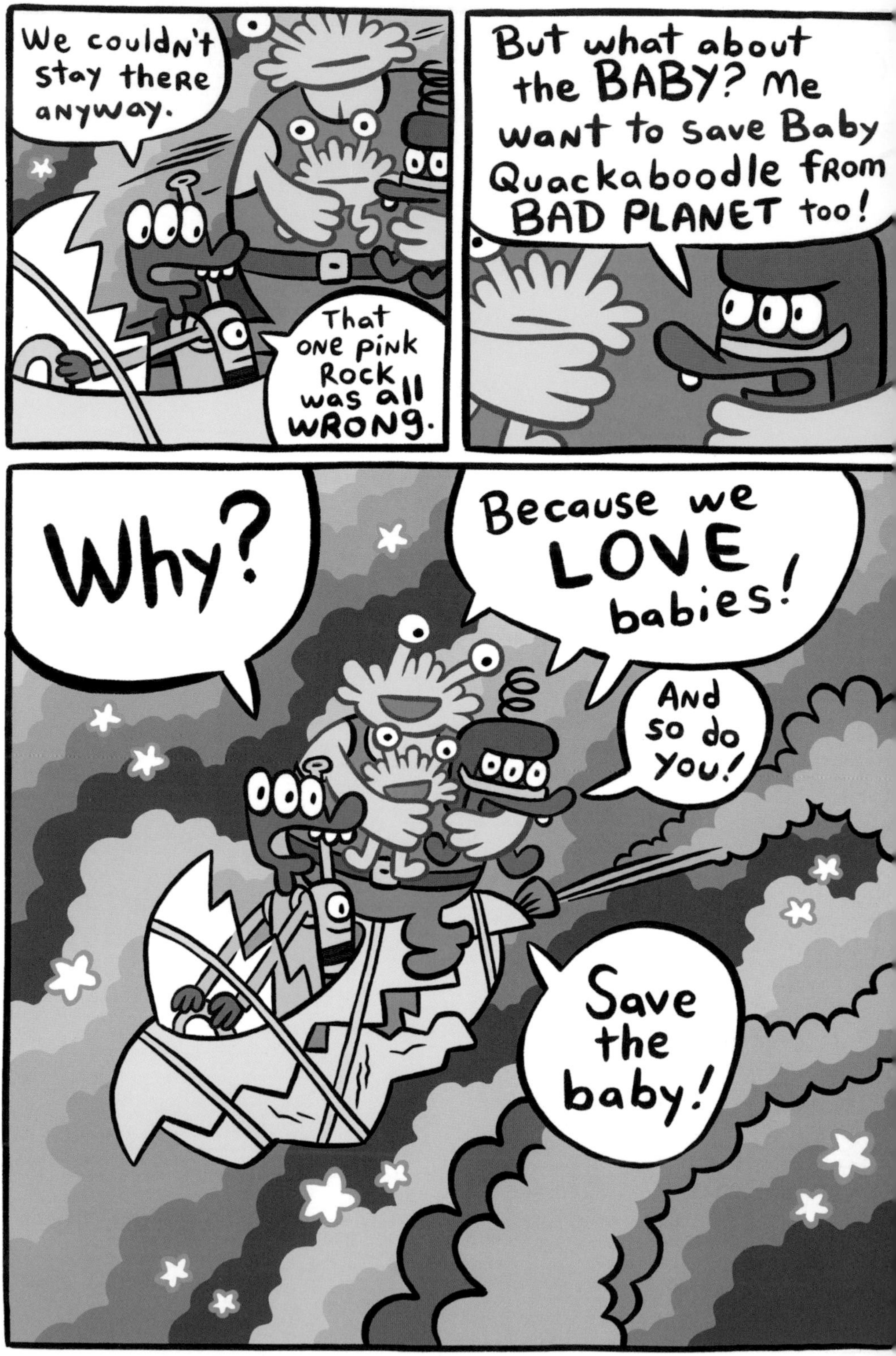
We couldn't stay there anyway.
That one pink Rock was all WRONG.
But what about the BABY? Me want to save Baby Quackaboodle from BAD PLANET too!
Why?
Because we LOVE babies!
And so do you!
Save the baby!

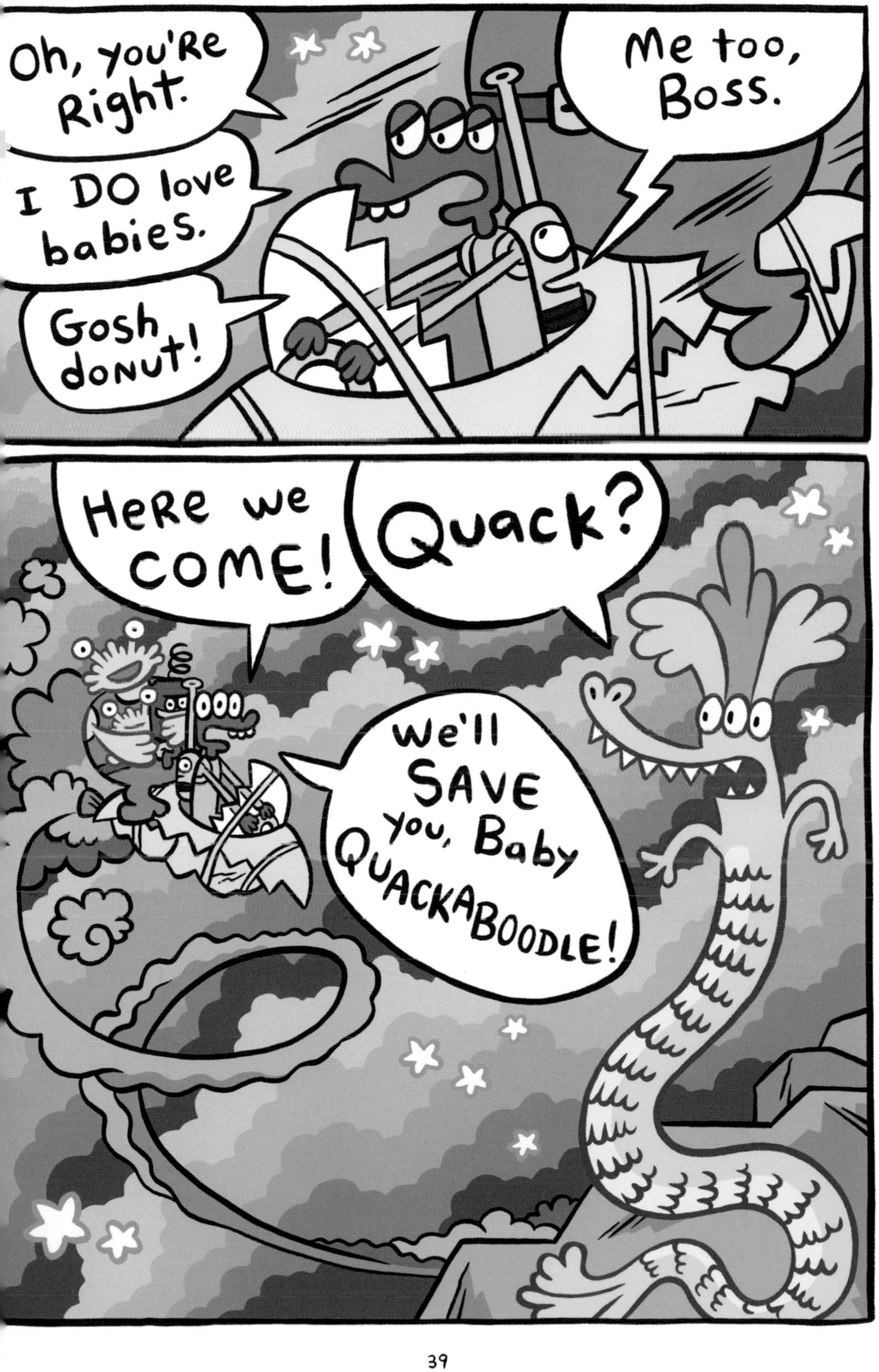
Oh, you're Right.
I DO love babies.
Gosh donut!
Me too, Boss.
Here we COME!
Quack?
We'll SAVE you, Baby QUACKABOODLE!

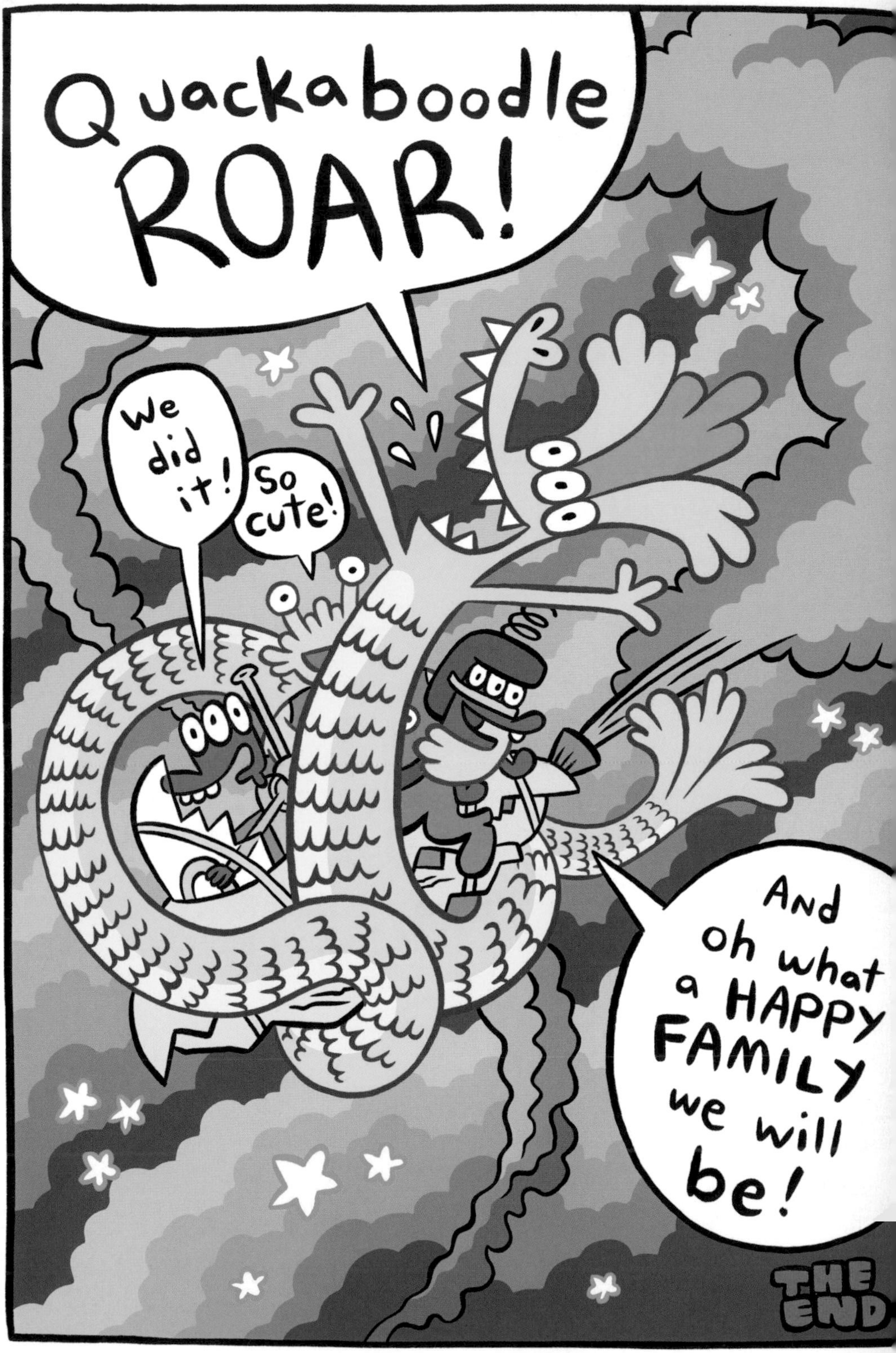
Quackaboodle ROAR!
We did it!
So cute!
And oh what a HAPPY FAMILY we will be!
THE END